T0166379

The Traveler's Tree

THE
TRAVELER'S TREE

BRUNO BONTEMPELLI

Translated by Linda Coverdale

The New Press · New York

1994

Published in the United States by The New Press, New York
Distributed by W. W. Norton & Company, Inc.,
500 Fifth Avenue, New York, NY 10110

Originally published in French as *L'Arbre du voyageur*
by Editions Grasset & Fasquelle, Paris, France, in 1992.
Copyright © 1992 by Editions Grasset & Fasquelle.

Library of Congress Cataloging-in-Publication Data

Bontempelli, Bruno.
[Arbre du voyageur. English]
The traveler's tree/Bruno Bontempelli; translated
by Linda Coverdale.
p.   cm.
ISBN 1–56584–150–6
1. French—Travel—Caribbean Area—
History—18th century—Fiction.
2. France—History, Naval—18th century—Fiction.
I. Coverdale, Linda. II. Title.
PQ2662.06245A7313   1994
843'.914—dc20   94–14818
                                  CIP

Book design by Charles Nix

Established in 1990
as a major alternative to the large,
commercial publishing houses,
The New Press is
the first full-scale nonprofit American book publisher
outside of the university presses.
The Press is operated editorially in the public interest,
rather than for private gain;
it is committed to publishing in innovative ways
works of educational, cultural, and community value
that, despite their intellectual merits,
might not normally be "commercially" viable.
The New Press's editorial offices
are located at the City University of New York.

Printed in the United States of America

94 95 96 97   9 8 7 6 5 4 3 2 1

"These, no doubt, were
singular fancies
to occupy a man's mind
in such extremity—
and I have often thought since,
that the revolutions
of the boat
around the pool
might have rendered me
a little light-headed."

—*A Descent into the Maelström*
EDGAR ALLAN POE

Note on Units of Measure

The French fathom of the old charts
is equal to 5 feet 3 inches,
or 1.624 meters.

A toise
is a measure equaling about 2.13 yards,
or 1.95 meters.

A cable's length
is about 213 yards,
or 195 meters.

Chapter

I.

THE *ENTREMETTEUSE** WALLOWED in the swell.
At dawn, the winds had fled, leaving the sultry air lying
heavily over that churning water. All morning long, the
sun had been a mere white smudge in the gray glare of
the sky.

It was two o'clock in the afternoon. Holding on to his
tricorn hat with one hand and gripping the rail with the
other, Saint-Foin was crossing the quarterdeck. The ship's
surgeon had come this way to avoid the rank smell that
permeated the lower deck, as he had no desire for more
than his fair share of that stench. He also hoped that a
breath of air, muggy though it was, might relieve the abdominal pain that had returned in the course of digestion.

Around him swirled a racket of tackle and sails, the
noisy commotion of fifty men lining the yards or clus-
tered about the rigging, busily reefing the topsails. There
was movement everywhere, and the *flûte*—it was a large

---

* The *Go-between*

storeship of seven hundred tons burden—grunted and swung round in all directions like an ox harried by wolves.

A treacherous lurch sent Saint-Foin staggering. Looking up suddenly, he saw the huge mass of spars cleave the air. As the ship rolled, he waved his arms and bobbed his head so vigorously that his hat flew overboard.

Only the cabin boy noticed the surgeon's groan of exasperation; the lad's mocking laughter, a falsetto cackle that sounded like sobbing, was cut short by a box on the ears from a sailor.

Saint-Foin watched his tricorn drift away.

"Goddam sea!" he thought disgustedly. "Next she'll be wanting our trouser buttons!"

He readjusted his white wig and proceeded cautiously forward, keeping a wary eye on the mint-green waves laced with strands of glairy spume.

Reaching the mainmast, he threaded his way through the men and the taut ropes, grasped the handrail, and descended the short, steep ladder leading to the waist. This long, open section of the deck between the fore cabin and the quarterdeck resembled a low courtyard protected by oaken walls. Secured there were the ship's guns as well as her small craft, reduced at present to the longboat and the jolly. Lying about were chains, bales of straw, and a large coop that had once held poultry. A faint odor of manure still lingered. This area was less crowded. Saint-Foin passed only a few men resting off in the corners, smoking, belching, snoring. He stepped over one youth lying in his own vomit, shaken by spasms. Skirting a puddle of wine, he entered the fore cabin.

Although the large galley oven stood not two steps away, the surgeon knew that it was not the source of the sticky heat now enveloping him, for the cook had let his fires go out. The cook was a big fellow with a coachman's mustache, but all Saint-Foin could see of him, as he sat on a barrel facing a scullion wiping out kettles, was his red turban and naked, sooty back. He was greedily gulping down great spoonfuls of skilly from a black mess tin.

"So the man still has the heart to gorge himself," thought the surgeon. "He must be made of stern stuff to stomach that revolting stew, and tolerate this abominable fetor! Doesn't he smell the stink of death about the ship?"

The heat persisted beyond the galley, as Saint-Foin had expected, but the odor of burned grease and boiled beans gave way to something more dreadful still.

"Yes," he murmured, "death…"

Situated all the way forward, beyond the capstan and the foremast, the sick bay was usually confined to a small dispensary closed off by bulkheads, thus affording easy access to the doors opening onto the head, that platform-grating out in the open prow where the crew relieved themselves and washed their laundry. These bulkheads now stretched completely athwartships. Entering through the central door, one saw fifteen cots occupied by fifteen half-naked men. The stench was here. It slopped about like oil, carefully contained by the closed portholes. Two hanging lamps swayed above the cots, the scuttlebutt, the guns stowed fore and aft along the ship's side, and the huge shaft of the iron-banded bowsprit that passed through the deck.

Saint-Foin stopped just inside the entrance. He did not glance at any of the patients. He looked around immediately for his assistant, Robinot, whom he spied across the room applying a plaster to a patient's leg.

To master his queasiness, Saint-Foin took a deep breath, like a swimmer plunging boldly into cold water. He recognized at once, beneath the acrid, pestilential smell, that sweetish odor he so feared. He shook himself.

"Robinot!" he called. "Why haven't you opened the ports?"

His assistant did not pause in his work.

"Sea's too high," he replied curtly.

The surgeon shrugged. From time to time, when the ship fell into a trough and seemed to touch a rocky bottom, they heard the heavy slap of a wave against the sheathing and a furious rush of water.

He was already stifling in the heat. He pulled out his handkerchief to wipe his neck, then walked along the row of cots, steadying himself here and there against the stanchions supporting the planking overhead. He looked at no one, and no one called out to him. They watched him silently. They knew where he was going.

He repressed a sudden desire to turn around and go back to his cabin.

"Would it make any difference?" he wondered.

He stopped at the sixth cot on the right.

The Traveler's Tree

A man lay there flat on his back, staring vacantly. He breathed with great difficulty, in hoarse little gasps. He wore only a pair of short drawers, sodden with sweat and loathsome humors. His entire body was covered with bluish spots and tubercles that oozed liquid like crushed raspberries.

Saint-Foin went over to him. There was a violent stink of diarrhea and pus, and that sickening sweetish smell. The surgeon touched the man's skin, as gray and bumpy as beech bark. He ran his fingers up to the face, where a scraggly beard parted to reveal a fissure lined with purplish-blue granulations, gummy with saliva. Bending over that opening, Saint-Foin caught a whiff of rotting meat. The few brown teeth still anchored within were swallowed up by puffy gums leaking serous fluid.

Feeling Saint-Foin's hand palpating his jaw, the man, without moving his head, turned crazed eyes upon the surgeon, who quickly withdrew his fingers. The salivary glands were enormous.

"Robinot! Did he take his Venice treacle?"

"No," replied the assistant without looking around. "Wouldn't this morning, either."

"You're not helping us much, my friend," Saint-Foin told the dying man.

"This one has cast us off," he thought. "He no longer believes in our remedies and doubts he will live to make old bones. He prefers to take the case himself, leaving everything to his own fear. Inside him the alarm bell is clanging like mad..."

"Has he taken a bit of broth?"

"Won't have that either. This monkey won't take but water. He smacks his lips to show he's thirsty."

Saint-Foin turned to the patient in the next cot.

"You, can you walk?"

"More like limping," began the man. "My foot—"

"Then you can get to the scuttlebutt. Give him all he wants to drink."

"Of that water?"

"Yes, of that water! I haven't any other, either for you or for him. You will add a shot of tafia to each mug, as you do for yourself. And you had better not scrimp on it, by God!"

Saint-Foin walked off, irritably brushing away flies. "Besides," he reflected, "what can that rotten mouth still taste? Foul water in foul flesh…"

He went over to a table set against the side of the ship, not far from Robinot. He removed his gray coat lined with crimson and hung it from a peg, carelessly pulled off his wig, tossed that on the peg as well, and unbuttoned his waistcoat. Then he sat down heavily on the stool in front of the table, which was covered with potions and instruments.

Fatigue weighed on his drooping eyelids and pendulous, old-dog jowls. He thought about his patient, sinking fast, already beyond his help. The man was going to die, perhaps within the hour, and this exasperated Saint-Foin. It was like the loss of his hat—the fury of impotence. Admittedly, his remedies were not panaceas, but was there not, in whatever ruled that still-living flesh, something capable of taking his efforts into account and being moved by them? Did everything depend solely on their arsenal of drugs? Deuce take it! Was there nothing, after all, but this vile mischief that snatched away a man as easily as a hat?

He stared without seeing at the scales, the mortars, pots, sifters, strainers. Enclosed by the raised edges of the table, this equipment was laid out upon a folded cloth soiled with greasy spots and dribbles of powder. On the left, the large medicine chest sat open, its compartments removed. Mismatched glass stoppers rattled in the necks of the case-bottles.

The ship plunged, startling him. Blinking, he felt a pang in his belly but chose to ignore it. He looked into a small porcelain crucible in which Robinot had prepared two ounces of green powder to be used on mouth ulcers. Pulling out his handkerchief to wipe his face, he turned to his assistant.

"Have you already administered the green powder?"

"Not yet."

"How far along are you?"

"I'm just finishing with this one. I have to apply another plaster over there, prepare some purgative, and bleed these three buggers here, who are not so far gone."

"I will handle the bloodletting," said Saint-Foin, waving away more flies.

Bracing his hands on his knees, he rose from the stool, picked up a lancet and three basins that he stacked one inside the other, and walked along the row of cots, swaying as the ship rolled.

The sick bay had been quiet until then. Beneath the

rumble of the sea one heard only the creaking of cots and the men clearing their throats. They lay in the stupor of a herd penned in a scorching barn, the numbness of fever and sweltry shadows, the almost listless attention of the body in pain. They would scratch themselves, the sleepers as well as the rest, and turn onto their backs, their sides, their stomachs. Occasionally someone would drag himself to the scuttlebutt to drink a swallow of its putrid water. That was all. Only two or three men still felt hearty enough to smoke their cutties, and the pungent smoke helped mask the pervasive stench.

The next patient Saint-Foin visited was one of these smokers. He had pale eyes and a thick thatch of gray hair half covering an earring. The hand holding the pipe to his mouth was missing the little finger. When the surgeon decided to bleed him at the ankle, the patient stuck out a leg deformed by bluish swellings on the calf. The foot was puffy and the skin speckled, stretched tight to bursting.

The man did not flinch when the lancet bit, but the sight of his blood disturbed him. He drew on his pipe before speaking.

"Is the island still there, Major?"

Saint-Foin was neither a major nor even a military man. The title was a simple whim on the part of the crew, who had similarly conferred the rank of commander to another man on board, the Chevalier Du Mouchet.

"Never fear," replied the surgeon. "She is still in sight. Do not move, and take care to keep your foot over the basin."

He straightened up, watched the basin for a moment to see that it would not tip with the ship's motion, and moved on to the next cot.

There lay a stout man, propped up on one elbow. A black beard grew high on his cheeks, and the bushy growth around his lips was flecked with saliva, as though he'd been glutting himself on cream.

"How far away do they say she is?" he asked.

Saint-Foin glanced at the edema, the swollen feet, the purple discoloration beneath the matted chest hair. He set down a basin, grabbed a forearm, and brandished his lancet.

"About forty miles," he replied, piercing the skin.

The man had winced under the knife. He relaxed, looking straight ahead.

"Bah," he exclaimed. "A good fresh wind and we reach her tomorrow."

From the adjacent cot rose a deep voice, cold and grave.

"Aye! But the only wind up now is blowing from the seat of your trousers."

There was no reply, for the bearded man could think of none. Although he would have liked to make a withering response, his indignation disarmed him, so he settled for a haughty look. Why quibble, when fortune was finally smiling on them?

Saint-Foin moved on to bleed the deep-voiced man. This one was tanned and gaunt. A long scar ran across his chest, from one black nipple to the opposite armpit.

He had not spoken since his one remark. He lay stiffly on his cot and greeted the stab of the lancet with perfect disdain, as though the operation were too minor to warrant even the slightest protest. Saint-Foin tried not to notice, yet he felt a kind of icy despair radiating from the man. He looked at him. That was worse. There was nothing to be done. He retreated.

Lancet in hand, he walked between the rows of cots for a moment before returning to his three patients.

"What of it?" he thought. "Am I responsible for this pestilence? Have I failed in my duty? Am I to blame if this damned voyage seems to go on forever? I cannot work miracles. I cannot cure all ills with a splash of holy water. If this disease is beyond us—them and me both—let them blame their own bodies, the Good Lord, Du Mouchet, or whomever they please! But not their surgeon, not Saint-Foin, who cannot hope to check such overwhelming disaster..."

Whiffs of the sweetish odor assailed his nostrils. It seemed to ooze from the dropsical swellings, the tubercles, the violine gums, the flaccid wounds abandoned to the air and the flies. He sensed the hidden workings of the flesh. He could imagine the itching that would result. The evidence was before his eyes, for the men would unconsciously scratch themselves, one after another, like a tribe of monkeys. Here a hand picked at the lips of a wound; there, fingernails scraped away at a dressing. This pruritus was relentless. When flesh grew torpid, when smarting remedies lost their bite, there was still the irritation of flies, the sting of sticky sweat, the rasp of coarse linen, the nip of a flea, or the sly stab of a mosquito, whose poison seemed to go on prickling forever.

A wizened and quite filthy little man near Saint-Foin suddenly sat bolt upright like a fiend.

"Major, I'm shitting blood!" he exclaimed. "Just a while ago, I shat some blood. Not that it frights me if blood runs from my nose or mouth. Look here! Even this accursed wound on my arm—I say to hell with that as well. Let it eat into me, spitting pus as it pleases. I swear to you, I don't give a damn..."

His speech was distorted by spittle, as though his mouth were stuffed with cotton wadding.

"But bleeding down there—Holy Mother! I don't want to die like that. You must plug me up, Major. I'm running out at the bottom! I'm like a leaky barrel, d'you understand? Listen, d'you understand?"

Saint-Foin understood perfectly. On the other hand, he did wonder why the fellow had sprung unexpectedly to life. Had he been asleep until then? Was he mad?

"Robinot, what have we given this man?"

His assistant was dabbing a patient's mouth with a cloth dipped in green powder.

"Rhubarb, cream of tartar," he replied, looking around for a moment. "And laudanum when he came in from the head in that condition."

"Has he slept?"

"Dear God, of course!"

"Good. No more purgatives. We'll give him simply some Venice treacle and a mug of seawater."

"And the laudanum?"

"I'll take care of that."

Saint-Foin went to his table, removed a flask of poppy syrup from the chest, and returned to administer a dose to the man, who was still muttering.

"When were you bled?"

"This morning. 'Twas yourself did it, Major, d'you not remember?"

"Well, we'll bleed you again this evening."

"Do as you like. Stick me like a pig an' it pleases you. I'd rather be bled a dozen times a day than drain out my own bunghole. That I don't want. Damnation take the rest! D'you understand, Major? The rest, this wound and everything—the hell with it…"

Saint-Foin turned his back on the man, but was pursued by his ranting. It took the brutal intervention of his neighbor to quiet the fellow, who broke off as abruptly as he had begun.

After putting away the poppy syrup, Saint-Foin went to bandage his three patients. Then he returned to empty the basins into a bucket, at the bottom of which lay a kind of revolting clotted whey mixed with congealed blood. The sweetish smell immediately overwhelmed him, and his stomach heaved violently. For a moment he thought he might vomit. He told himself he must not vomit into that slop. He had moved back a few paces, and still the odor persisted. He withdrew all the way to the table without shaking it off. It was intolerable. He had to empty that bucket.

He picked it up by the rope handle and went out to the

head. Stepping onto the grating, he tipped the bucket over the rail, shaking it for a long time before lowering it down the side to be rinsed by the waves.

The sea smashed against the bow and swept up over the platform, quickly soaking Saint-Foin's shoes and stockings, but he welcomed this water that washed away his nausea.

The ship pitched and rolled. He stood straddling, gripping the headrail. Before him was the rough-hewn back of the figurehead, swinging stiffly about like a wooden rocking horse. Above it soared the colossal bowsprit, all rigged out with shrouds and martingales. He breathed in the fine spindrift, surrendering himself to the vertiginous plunging of the ship and the crashing waves.

He stood there a while, thinking of nothing, staring out at the rough sea. He looked in vain for the island, but was not alarmed by its absence.

"The ship has come about," he thought. "The isle must lie somewhere behind me. Without any wind, it would take a fearsome current to whisk us from her. The danger is past. It was during the night we might have lost her."

It was already quite late when they had spotted her the evening before. Twelve days at sea with the horizon running flat and empty like a clean plate. And the previous landfall a mere pebble. A sight for sore eyes, last night, true enough...

"When he steered for her, Bloche knew that darkness was waiting to steal the prize. A fine race against sundown, Captain! Despite the swell and the shifting winds...

But lost at the outset. There is no dusk, no twilight in these parts; night falls as one piece. And suddenly the island vanished. Heave to, or go blindly on, peering at the compass? All the same. Fate was toying with us, and there was nothing to do but wait…"

He recalled the nerve-racking wait for daybreak, the cry from a topman, and then, at first light, the whispering of the crew, a murmur that had swelled and then exploded when the island appeared out of the blue. The winds had sighed and moaned that night; their flight left the ship's company dazed, blissful, delighted to have blundered upon this scrap of land, and to enjoy it even from afar. Relieved of their impatience, they had ample time to savor their longing.

"Yes, this island will rescue us…I swear that upon my return I shall cling to dry land and never leave it again. I shall take care of gouty burghers, attend their wives and daughters in childbed…"

His thoughts were interrupted when a patient stepped through the other door to relieve himself. Seeing the surgeon, the man hesitated, but his need was urgent. He crouched over the opposite hole, steadying himself with one hand, and hastily did his business. Then he popped back inside without a word.

Saint-Foin's nose was on the alert, fearing possible offense, but the odor of the man's evacuation did not waft across the bow. The surgeon lingered, enjoying his mild giddiness and the delicious scent of the sea. He was now soaked to the knees, and in places his shirt clung wetly to his skin. The pain in his abdomen had faded to a slight stitch in one spot. He had managed to settle his back against the ship's side and was half-sitting on a narrow slat. Between his feet lay one of the two privy holes. Beneath, the water boiled with foam. He dozed.

After spending almost an hour out in the bows, Saint-Foin picked up the bucket and returned to the sick bay.

He sensed at once that the silence was different, attentive. Ears strained to catch the painful rasp of shallow breathing, of lungs struggling desperately for air.

Saint-Foin saw his assistant standing motionless by the table. He understood. He looked over at the dying man.

The sufferer's spine was arched, his head thrown back, the jaws working. He was suffocating. His whole body strained along with that stinking mouth as it gulped at emptiness. The only sounds were the sucking of mucous membranes and a dreadful hissing of saliva. The man did not speak; his eyes were closed. It was the end, and he let it buffet him without believing what was happening. His eyelids were so smooth that he seemed calm in the depths of his terror.

Death came, but with a strange gentleness. Without a single grimace, the man sank slowly back onto his cot, his mouth still agape, a creamy thread trickling from one corner across his gray cheek.

No one had lifted a finger, least of all Saint-Foin, who knew any aid was useless. "We'll save the rest of them," was all he thought; and then: "Bloche must be informed."

Next, breaking into the mixture of horror and contemplation that paralyzed the others, he gave an order.

"Robinot, go fetch some men to take the body out on deck. He'll be stinking horribly before very long."

Brutal words, but Saint-Foin hardly concerned himself with sparing the patients' feelings. Besides, who among them did not already know that the rotting of his flesh was a foretaste of his own death?

Saint-Foin slipped his coat back on, stuffed his wig into a pocket, and searched briefly for his tricorn before recalling that he had lost it to a bad lee-lurch.

He left, resolutely choosing the most direct path: across the main deck. Emerging from the whirlpool of heat in the waist, he stepped beneath the quarterdeck. Shadows moved about; he did not see them. He did not notice the stench, only the inoffensive smells of tar and aged wood. Walking around the shaft of the mainmast, the main capstan, and the ladder, he made his way through a jumble of casks, chests, baskets bristling with ailing plant cuttings, and piles of cages housing listless birds. He saw poorly in the faint light shed by the hatch overhead. There was straw underfoot. He knocked into crates and sacks. Suddenly, one of these bumps sent two feathered rockets aloft with a great squawking. His heart leaped. They were two parrots who had escaped from their cage and now fluttered their startling colors around him. Recovered from his surprise, Saint-Foin watched them thoughtfully. Behind him, the open sky of the waist should have proved irresistible...

"What are you waiting for?" he called to them. "Off with you, silly buggers, while you still can!"

But the birds hung back. Saint-Foin dismissed them with a wave and went on his way.

He entered the dark central corridor flanked by the staff officers' cabins. He passed his own door and those of his companions. Silence. Behind the small panels floated the torpors of the siesta, idle reverie, or the distracted hesitation of a hand poised over a blank page in a journal. At the end of the passage he pushed through a double door and stepped into the great cabin.

He was greeted by a burst of bright light. Three of the stern-gallery windows were open, admitting the sound of waves. The stale smell of stew mixed with the odors of wax and salt spray. Two brass hanging lamps swung above the large table, cheeping like birds. To the right, a few of the sea charts cluttering the desk had fallen to the deck. Everything else was in order: the chairs upholstered in red, the fringe on the rug, the muskets in the gun rack—even the pictures hung evenly. Saint-Foin had never before been as keenly aware of the cabin's general air of a rustic retreat, a luxurious refuge from all the vagaries of misfortune. This feeling of safety was suddenly so vivid that he found himself wishing, "Oh, to stay here forever!"

At first he saw only a servant collecting candle stumps in a towel. Then, behind him, seated at the table, he noticed Cornelius Trinquet. The old man was leaning over a bowl, dabbing at one eyelid with a handkerchief soaked in a glaucous liquid, most of which ran down his cheek and back into the bowl while the rest dribbled under his chin, into a cloth he held against his throat.

At the sight of that nasty potion, against which he had already warned Trinquet, Saint-Foin felt a twinge of irritation, but he had more pressing concerns. He merely asked if the captain was in his quarters. The captain's small cabin opened off the great cabin, on the starboard side; its companion on the opposite side belonged to the first mate.

Trinquet looked up with one red, swollen eye; the compress covered the other. His gray hair hung limply against his ashen cheeks. He paused before answering, as though in protest at the brusqueness of the question.

"No," he replied at last. "Why the great hurry?"

"And Girandole?"

"They left together. What is going on?"

Saint-Foin hesitated. He suddenly found everything about Trinquet exasperating: his wizened face, his old-clothes smell, his absurd witches' brew, his disdain for the ship, for the care and effort required to run her well...

"Isn't he the most to blame?" thought Saint-Foin.

He withdrew without telling him what had happened.

Going back the way he had come, he climbed the ladder and emerged onto the quarterdeck in front of the mizzen-mast and the wheel, just as he had two hours earlier. The sky was washed with the same luminous, chalky white, against which shivered the sails still set upon their yards. The ship's capers made the rigging creak and raised lazy puffs of air. There was still some activity aloft. Men clambered up the ratlines, and one petty officer, perched in a top, ordered his people about with great bellowing.

Saint-Foin turned to the helmsman, impassive in his red cap, with nothing to do but keep a weather eye out for the slightest breath of wind. Four steps behind him was the breastwork of the quarters that the Chevalier Du Mouchet had had constructed for himself for this voyage and which spanned the entire width of the quarterdeck. A solid door opened onto the deck; a thick festoon and the three stern-lanterns crowned the cabin at the aft end.

Once again, Saint-Foin hesitated.

"Should I rouse the chevalier? What good would that do? The news would distress him, and after sending me on to Bloche, he would resume his nap. Well, then, why make a fuss? The news will spread quickly enough. In the meantime, let Bloche deal with it."

Saint-Foin approached the helmsman, who had just bitten off a chew from a plug of tobacco, and asked him where the captain was. The man thrust out his chin in reply: forward, through the maze of the rigging, the massive black silhouette of Captain Bloche could be seen looming at the forecastle rail with his first mate, Girandole, by his side. They were watching four sailors hoist a body wrapped in a sheet up the ladder from the waist.

The burial service was held at six in the evening, beneath a sky flushed with mauve. The *flûte* still groaned as she heaved on the swell; now and again her slack sails snapped like flags.

The seventy-odd seamen had stationed themselves

aloft, and on the forecastle, the quarterdeck, in the waist, and along the gangways. Despite their grave demeanor, every one of them was now confident he would escape this miserable end. Oh, some other death might carry a man off at any moment, swelling the roll of those shipmates lost along the way—but, heaven be praised, *he* would not die like this. They had outstripped this rotting sickness. Only one of them had let himself be overtaken. Bad luck, true enough—even damnable bad luck, within the very sight of salvation!

A single person was missing from the group of gentlemen and officers assembled by the mainmast. Picot-Fleury, the naturalist, was ill. Next to the stout figure of Captain Bloche stood the Chevalier Du Mouchet—*in extenso,* Jacques-Honorat Pinson Du Mouchet—wearing boots, a tricorn trimmed with braid, a gray coat, and his sword, hanging from a shoulder belt. Behind them was the hydrographer, Cornelius Trinquet, buttoned up tight in an old justaucorps with large, gaping pockets, his eyes reddened by chronic inflammation. The ship's writer, Malestro, in black hat and boots, stood coldly by with crossed arms. Finally, there was Saint-Foin, who had found a spare tricorn, and the three senior officers: the first mate, Girandole; the second mate, Montpassé; and the third mate, young Colinet. Two other comrades ought to have been among this company, but misfortune had a month earlier carried off the expedition's artist, Vuché de Beaune, and Lieutenant Comblezac.

The corpse was sewn up in a piece of sailcloth weighted with two six-pound cannonballs. The body lay before the gangport on the plank furnished, according to custom, by the ship's cook.

The captain began his speech, which was tricked out with a few bits and pieces of dog Latin. Meanwhile, the sky got under way. High overhead gathered an ash-gray flock, their big bellies edged with ocher. Turbulence in the west melted into transparencies of honey and coral. Gold-fringed curtains slowly parted to release exuberant greens, chrome and sulfur yellows.

At the end of the service, the great bell at the forecastle was struck. All present doffed hats and caps for a moment of meditation. The heavens were now teeming with a whole migration toward the blazing sunset: rosy eiderdown, wisps of brown smoke, strings of little bundles accented with saffron, shawls, blond-wood shavings, shreds and ribbons, twisted lengths of muslin, shovelfuls of lavender snow, and bringing up the rear, dove-gray tufts still escaping from the leaden twilight. This flashing excess had flared up suddenly around the sun, which sank into the breach, spilling a dazzling stream across the sea. The water now resembled cut glass of a very pale green.

At a sign from the captain, four men lifted the plank to the edge of the gangport and tipped it up. The rough cloth slid across the wood. The sun sank redly, cooling like a piece of wrought iron. The clouds were now freighted with purple, and a vast slate-colored shadow, a wave of soot and ashes, was putting out the sky.

Plummeting from the motionless ship, the sack went straight to the bottom.

Chapter

II.

NIGHT SPREAD OUT like a feather bed. The sea was still stirring, but something heavy was settling upon the waters, quieting them. The *flûte* no longer flung her stern about; she glided slowly along in a stately pavane, drawing out the figures of her dance like a huge ballerina. At midnight, her languid movement was no more than the gentlest swaying on a sea of milk.

This rocking lulled the seamen's slumber into the deep. They gave themselves up gratefully to their fatigue. The hammock ropes stopped squeaking; the creaking of wood and rigging died away; the only sound throughout the ship was like the gulping of a cow at the water trough. Before dawn, the sea had gone perfectly smooth.

The men awoke dazed by this intoxicating calm. They became insubstantial creatures, their minds all clouded over with dreams of water. The silence was immense. The ship seemed stranded in the middle of a desert. Only the faint grating of woodworms, a man's footsteps on deck, and the drowsy buzz of a fly...

It was a disquieting silence. A few men slipped from their hammocks to peer out of the scuttles. They saw nothing but grayness, black water, and the vaguest of horizons. Where was the island?

First, find the west. There, that murkiness going all rainbow-colored, that's the east. The island lies to the west...So she must be on the bows—worse luck. No use twisting your head off. Can't be seen from here. Ahoy! You on the other side, have you spotted her?...Nay, but we can't see a thing. We'll have to go topside...

A few decided to wait until sunrise and returned to their hammocks. The others went up to join the watch, all grouped around Montpassé in the bows. The second mate was scanning the soupy horizon with his spyglass. Up on the foretop with a few topmen, Colinet was doing the same. No one asked any questions, but everyone wondered whether this impenetrable molasses was night, fog, or a bit of both.

The eastern pallor of the sky streamed upward and finally reached the west, showing it to be wreathed after all in an impalpable mist.

The island still had not been sighted by the time Girandole came on watch. Since he saw no point in squinting at this fog indefinitely, he merely trained his glass upon it from time to time. That is how, at half past five, he spied two large black birds to the northwest. They were a pair of frigates, more interested in their fishing than in the ship, which they approached only in the course of their aerobatics. Sometimes they dropped like stones, vanishing into the low-lying haze before reaching the water.

After a while they could be seen with the naked eye. Their presence rekindled hope. Everyone gazed at these two black scraps of ribbed silk torn off from the island. When they were close enough for those on deck to see their red crops, they abandoned their fishing and swept in for a reconnaissance. One pass was enough. They flew quite high over the rigging and disappeared off to the south.

Solitude weighed on the men once again. Smooth, the ocean appeared even more deserted. To the crushing immensity of water and sky was added this uncanny silence of the morning twilight, a strangeness not like death but like the dawn of creation. At first, daybreak was entangled in layers of clouds, but then the sun hoisted itself above them and began to light up the entire sky. The last gray shadows gave way to pure blue. To the west, shafts of garish light burned off the mist. Now, on the keen edge of the horizon, appeared the small notch of the island.

A great brightness had awakened the chevalier, flooding his eyelids with poppy red. In the night, he had imagined that he was being carried by an enormous tumbrel running alongside a torrent, but now the silence swallowed up all sound, save for a faint intermittent creaking. He half-opened his eyes. A brilliant light was splattering the cabin with little squares of a vivid daffodil color. The hanging brass lamp sparkled. The pommel of his sword gleamed upon the table, where he had tossed it the night before, along with the shoulder belt and the tricorn of gray felt. This dazzling yellow from the gallery windows was splashed over the console table, the chest, the portolano, the mahogany writing desk, the two pistols in their rack, and the Turkish scene hanging opposite the mirror.

He tipped his head back to see the sky, but the fierce glare burned his eyes. Grimacing, he rested for a moment on the pillow. His stomach was bothering him. Mingling with the odor of candlewax was a moldy, dirty-clothes smell of fermenting sweat. He rose from his cot.

He put on his drawers, his shirt (letting the jabot hang untied), his white stockings, his knee breeches; he painfully drew on his top boots, rang for his servant, and went to open the door of the gallery.

The sun had risen above the dense haze to the east. The sky overhead was a hard, empty blue. Not one breath of air on that motionless sea.

He unbuttoned the front flap of his breeches and urinated into the water fifteen feet below. There was no trace of a wake; the ship was still becalmed. Buttoning himself up, he wondered how far they were from Caine. He stayed on the balcony for a while, thinking of his home.

This homeland, set around the great bay discovered a century earlier by the navigator Calicueva de Caine, was a mere nick in the wilderness. Facing the vastness of the ocean, it was the last link in a chain stretching from the Old World. True, men set out from there to explore, to plunder, to chart new islands, but those adventurers who returned—for many never did—had often sacrificed their campaigns of discovery or privateering to the soon pressing struggle for sheer survival. After its beginnings as a small fortified town, Caine had become a thriving community with its rich and its poor, its bourgeois and its buccaneers. The only thing missing was an aristocracy— a true one, that is, because there was a wealth of titles that had been called out of abeyance; indeed, Jacques's grandfather, Jean-Denis Pinson, had used his prestige as a shipowner to wangle the Du Mouchet barony for himself. And there the chevalier had lived, supported by a substantial fortune, in the customary indolence of tropic climes. His departure had astonished everyone. Nobody in Caine had understood his sudden passion for geography. They had taken it for a passing fancy; he had never wavered. Urged on by his former tutor, Cornelius Trinquet, who still treated him with easy familiarity, the chevalier had had one of his family's storeships fitted out at great expense, for he wished to sail on her with all the comforts of home. Quarters had been constructed for him aft on the quarterdeck, and on the main deck for his guests; portholes had been opened between decks. Then, with a large store of provisions on board, the *flûte* had set sail six months ago for the greater glory of Geography. Or was it, quite simply, for a change of scenery?...

Someone knocked on the small side door cut into what

appeared to be a cupboard and which opened onto a ladder to the deck below. A lame servant limped in with the breakfast tray.

"My respects, Commander," he said in a hoarse voice. "The island is still there, due west, right ahead."

Stepping into his narrow shaving closet, which was set above the officers' privy, the chevalier poured water into a basin and splashed some on his face.

"Well, then," he said. "I trust you are reassured."

"Pardi!" exclaimed the servant. "I am indeed."

Trailing the aroma of coffee, he crossed the cabin to begin setting the table.

"Mind you, at first light, there was so much fog, you couldn't make out a thing over where we'd last seen her."

"We are in the doldrums. What could possibly happen?"

"Currents and such like. Who knows! Islands, they steal away from you for no good reason, Commander. Remember all those that vanished into thin air."

"I remember."

The chevalier studied himself in the mirror. At forty, his face was a bit puffy, with slight bags under the eyes and tiny brown flecks on the dry skin of his lips. He still had very long lashes, however, and his dark eyes had not lost their luster. He decided against shaving cheeks so lightly shadowed.

"Here," continued the servant, "the one that had an islet so like, you would have taken them for mother and child. Do you remember? At nightfall, we were almost close enough to touch her. We could have picked daisies there."

"Had there been any," remarked the chevalier as he reentered the room, crossing to stand before the large mirror over the console.

He took up his white wig with both hands and plunked it down upon his head. Then he powdered the edges where they lay against his cheeks.

"And that one we bore down upon all night. Morning fog, contrary wind, and—farewell, my beauty. Even the captain couldn't believe it."

"What do you want? One cannot have them all...Is there any other news?"

"No, Commander...Good day, then, Commander," added the servant, who had completed his task and now left by the small side door.

The chevalier sat down at the table. He lifted the cup of coffee to his lips. He was not hungry, but welcomed the hot drink. He picked at the soft crumb of a hunk of bread and swallowed a spoonful of honey, which immediately made him feel sick.

He was poorly rested, both weary and on edge. Despite his nausea, he was thirsty and wanted something to suck on. He lighted one of his little green cigars and finished dressing. Then he left, descending the same ladder the servant had taken.

In the great cabin, he found portly Captain Bloche lolling in an armchair, his black waistcoat hanging open. With his fleshy lips set in a pout, he was morosely casting a fishy eye over the pages of a thick account book. The ship's writer, Malestro, stood off to one side at the chart table, poking idly around among the rolled-up maps. The two men greeted the chevalier, somewhat surprised to see him up at that hour.

Bloche set the book down on the table and drew a snuffbox from his waistcoat pocket. Then he rang a small bell, and stuffed some tobacco up his nostrils, which were narrow and delicately shaped.

"We are down to fifteen days of ship's biscuit," he said, "and ten of water. The dried vegetables and salt provisions are still abundant, but much spoiled, I fear. I shall have to take stock of this myself. We shall arrange an inspection together, Malestro."

"Prepare yourself for a distressing discovery," replied the other man. "The entire hold stinks."

Bloche made a face in silence. When the servant appeared, the captain asked for coffee.

"We are even running short of coffee. Only our wine stores are still plentiful. Meager fare. If we had had to make straight for Caine, we would not have made it alive. This island is a blessing, believe me."

"I do not doubt it," replied the chevalier dryly, crossing to the gallery windows.

The horizon was now a razor-sharp line. The chevalier could not see the island, but he knew it was out there, somewhere.

"Has Trinquet discovered what island it is?" he asked.

The captain started.

"Trinquet!" he exclaimed contemptuously. "Monsieur, you know full well that your hydrographer has taken his discharge along with all his paraphernalia. Since being torn away from his mission, he will have nothing more to do with us."

"Granted! But he might be able to shed some light upon this landfall."

"All that we might chance upon during our return voyage is of no concern to him. He devotes himself entirely to his scribbling, intended for his dear Ministry of Longitude."

"I wonder how he can, for he no longer sees at all."

"So he claims. I am not so sure his affliction is that advanced. The truth of it is, he cold-shoulders us and will no longer stick his nose in a map, either for you or for me. This morning he answered me, 'Islands? I have enough and to spare of them!' Whereupon he turned on his heel and left."

The chevalier felt it useless to defend Cornelius.

"And you, do you know where we are?"

"How should I? Monsieur Trinquet's chronometer has made a pretty mess of our longitudes. This so-called revolutionary device has served only to send us a-wandering. No, I do not know where we are. Rest assured, however, that we will reach Caine. By dead reckoning. 'Twill serve at least as well. Better to know that one does not know where one is than to believe one is where one is not."

The servant brought a coffee pot and some cups on a tray. Although the chevalier did not partake, he did sit down in one of the armchairs, where he lighted his second cigar.

The Traveler's Tree

The aroma of coffee spread throughout the cabin, but it was more promising than substantial: after it was boiled, the water still tasted rather foul and required much sugar to mask its bitterness. As for Malestro, he had accepted a cup and seated himself at the table. As usual, he wore his boots and his bronze velvet coat, which was quite threadbare. His long, greasy, jet-black hair was tied back at the nape. His face, crossed by a scar that wrinkled one eyelid, wore a perpetual and imperceptible smile.

Bloche asked him several questions about the provisions for the officers and gentlemen, receiving only evasive replies. Malestro merely remarked that he would consult Maringot, the ship's steward.

Then, draining his cup, he tucked the account book under his arm and withdrew.

The captain was pensive for a moment. So was the chevalier. They were both thinking the same thing.

"Upon my word," exclaimed Bloche at last, "I shall never get used to that man."

The chevalier smiled ironically.

"You are mistaken. I warrant he would have granted you a share of his spoils."

He was alluding to Malestro's secret investigations during the voyage, his schemes, his mysterious visits to the islands they visited, his daring expeditions into hostile territory. Although the man was extraordinarily close-mouthed, it had quickly become known that he nourished ambitions beyond that of serving their noble campaign. The most likely hypothesis was seized upon: he was searching for a treasure hidden away in some odd corner of the ocean. Someone claimed that he possessed a message found in a bottle. It was later learned, from a sailor who associated with wreckers in Caine (a common occupation in a country where debris from the most distant horizons was constantly washing up on shore), that Malestro had an understanding with them to buy all such bottles, paying cash on the spot, and that he had thus amassed a goodly number of them. The figures put forward were quite fanciful. Nevertheless, it was generally supposed that he had brought along more than one message and was tracking more than one prize. It was impossible to be certain of this, however, or to learn anything further. Malestro was as silent as the grave, and the two gunners he had taken up with—and just what did *they* know?—would have cut out their own tongues before saying a word. Sworn to silence? Intimidated? Perhaps both. Those two fellows were not the sort to be easily frightened, and there was no doubt Malestro was not stingy when his interests were at stake…

Girandole had arrived to report to the captain that the deep-sea lead had not found bottom at a hundred and twenty fathoms. Bloche made a note of this and offered him coffee. The first mate accepted a cup, which he drank standing, his tricorn under his arm.

Girandole seemed stiff and starchy beside the captain's informality, and a certain obsequious something in his eye and bearing immediately stamped him as a stickler for regulations.

"How far along are you with those repairs to the main topgallant mast?" asked Bloche.

"Monsieur de Montpassé has that in hand. I believe the mast will be sent up this afternoon."

"Good...good...And the fishing?"

"Not a bite."

"Those lines will not do. Send some men out in the longboat to seine for fish."

"As you wish, Captain. Ah, I wanted to tell you that some white birds passed within musket range. It would be well to post two or three men in case others should appear."

"Excellent suggestion, Girandole. But detail no one. I shall undertake this little task myself. It will be invigorating. You are on watch, are you not? Well, that is a pity. Monsieur Du Mouchet, will you accompany me?"

"Why not?"

"Good. I shall be with you in a minute."

Bloche rose heavily and shut himself into the privy in the starboard quarter-gallery. When he emerged, he was rebuttoning his breeches casually. He straightened his wig, which was too short for his plump face, adjusted his old black coat trimmed with white braid, fastened his waistcoat, clapped on his grease-stained tricorn, and removed two muskets from the gun rack. Then he stood aside to let the chevalier pass, following with that funny walk he had, stepping out smartly in his high boots.

*

The two kept watch in vain. Birds were scarce and out of range. Finally the hunters lost interest in them, as well as in the fishermen a cable's length away who were having trouble setting and hauling their net.

"Those imbeciles won't catch a thing," observed Bloche.

And he dragged the chevalier along with him to the other side of the ship, as much to avoid that sorry sight as to try their luck elsewhere.

In their slow progress they passed some men at work and others at leisure. The carpenters' hammering was echoed by a mallet pounding on a barrel. Two hands had sloshed pails of water on the planking and were now idly swabbing the deck. No orders, no shouts; occasionally, a man near the rail would call out to the fishermen. Distant voices would reply as though from across a field. The only sound in the limpid air was a feeble lapping of dead water.

They paused in the waist to look aloft at what was left of the main topgallant mast: two feet of wood stuck in the cap of the topmast. Then Bloche studied the rigging with a scowl.

His fishy eye, dull-looking yet sharp-sighted, took in all the wear and tear, the patchwork mending. There was much split wood and harsh groaning; many iron fittings were warped. The big square-rigged three-master, once as solid as a wooden shoe, had suffered cruelly from these six months at sea away from the dockyard. Now the *Entremetteuse* resembled an aged whale with a thousand aches and pains, gnawed at by worms and encrusted with barnacles.

They saw no birds on the other side and never got off a single shot. In the end they gave up, returning to the great cabin at dinner time.

The fare was a thin soup and a stew made of old salt pork and dried beans. These meals were becoming an ordeal. They fell back on the bitter bread, kneaded with seawater, but they refreshed themselves most of all with the excellent wine of Caine, with its delicate savor of figs. It was the only item among the gentlemen's provisions, along with a very old muscatel stored in half-liter bottles, to have improved during the voyage.

Saint-Foin informed those present that Picot-Fleury's condition had worsened. Fever and vomiting. During the night, his assistant, Dominique—a girlishly slender young man who slept in the naturalist's cabin—had disobeyed the sick man's orders and awakened the surgeon. Saint-Foin had found the patient utterly exhausted, drenched in sweat and splattered with spew, as he had been unable to reach a basin in time. These details spoiled what was left of the diners' appetites. The messmates soon went off to their siestas.

The afternoon wore on interminably. Those hands about their chores suffered from the heat; the others were stricken with a languor and a malaise they could not shake off, either standing up or lying down. Men shuffled along the deck, went below, and came back up again to seek a comfortable spot, like dogs turning round on a doormat.

The main topgallant mast was stepped. The fishermen had come back empty-handed.

The return of milder air that evening at first afforded much relief. Then, gradually, there came a feeling of crushing immobility. The pale purple haze reappeared. The island vanished into its muslin veils.

Until dawn, the ship's lanterns shone only upon stifling darkness, a warm, heavy sootiness that finally began paling to gray, turning slate-colored in the morning twilight. The island did not emerge from the mist until much later, slightly farther to the southwest. They thought the sky might grow threatening, but the rising sun turned the heavens the same porcelain blue as the day before. The sea was a sheet of breathless calm.

At dinner, the faces around the table were gloomy. Bloche noisily slurped his soup, in which he had set some pieces of bread to soak. He listened to Saint-Foin with an expression of disgust, although it was hard to tell whether it was what he was hearing or what he was eating that distressed him. The surgeon was speaking in some agitation.

"Two more arrived this morning. And I swear to you, the other fifteen are not a pretty sight. But this is nothing compared to what *could* befall us. You see, this disease progresses like an epidemic: one hand comes down with it; then ten, twenty others fall ill. One dead man leads the way, and the rest follow him pell-mell..."

Bloche listened quietly. When he was certain the surgeon had finished, he put down his spoon, looked across the table at the Chevalier Du Mouchet, then turned to his first mate.

"Your opinion, Girandole?"

"Indeed, time is running out for us, Captain. I see no other choice but to pull in with the longboat toward the island until we are within soundings. Then we may ply between ship and shore in the boats..."

"Are you aware the island lies a good fifteen leagues away?"

"If we make three leagues a day, perhaps four..."

"...We will bring all our able-bodied men to their knees."

"There is always the hope that in the meantime the wind may return."

Trinquet spoke up without looking away from his plate.

"You'll say 'tis none of my business, but why don't you send off the jollyboat? It could bring back the first fresh provisions."

"That would be two days lost," observed Saint-Foin curtly.

"I had thought of that," said Bloche, "and I admit to preferring this plan as being easier on the men."

"Easier!" exclaimed Saint-Foin. "Easier for whom, Captain? Do our sick men no longer count for anything in your eyes? Would you write them off? Do you already take them for dead?"

"You put me out of temper, Saint-Foin! Pulling this old tub is not child's play. 'Tis work for galley slaves, I tell you! And it is precisely to spare you any further customers that I shrink from choosing this course."

The discussion continued. They could not decide between pulling in or sending out the jolly; then someone suggested they might do both. After more discussion, and Bloche's decision to put the matter to a vote, this idea finally carried the day.

Montpassé volunteered to lead the expedition. Bloche accepted his offer. Six men and a bosun were to accompany the second mate, and the craft would be loaded with casks, along with muskets and a barrel of powder. As for the longboat, Bloche and the surgeon would select the rowers, who would set out at seven that evening.

"Why not earlier?" inquired Saint-Foin.

"Would you have our oarsmen, on top of all else, fried to a crisp?"

Intent on shaking some life into his crew, Bloche had ordered all remaining sail lowered, the deck swabbed, the hammocks made fast to the gantlines, all sea chests tidied, and he had warned his officers to show the utmost firmness in carrying out these commands.

The men had been lazily awaiting their dinner, which was really only a revolting skilly scooped from a tub; the coarse wine masked the flavor, and the tafia made up for the wine. Then they would have welcomed a long, lazy nap in some shady spot. Instead, here they were, toiling away like convicts. The afternoon began to blaze. The blue of the sky took on black and blinding depths. Overhead was a sunburst, an exploding shower that made the air burn and the ship steam. The iron fittings were white-hot, untouchable. Wetted down, the planking dried before their very eyes and soon was again hot enough to sear callused feet. Yet almost seventy men were toiling from stem to stern, as though preparing to dress ship.

Bloche had not imposed such labors without good reason. True, he thought it worthwhile to clean up the poor old bucket, but he wished above all to take the pulse of his crew. A sailor's health is not best judged when he is lolling about in the grip of the doldrums.

"What is troubling Saint-Foin?" he asked Girandole. "These people are holding up well enough. Of course, they must not be driven too hard. Oh, I know! Most of them are only half-alive, and the rest are half-dead. Well, what of it! A ship cannot sail on prayers. Everyone still on his feet will be put to the oars. Now is not the time for half-measures. Only those buggers who fail to pass muster will be exempted."

He already saw many signs of weakness and surliness in the men; some were sluggish at their work, struggling, even suffering. Some old hands made bold to send him dark, bitter looks that said, "Now we're to have *you* on our backs as well?"

"Prodromes!" exclaimed the captain. "Saint-Foin speaks to me of prodromes. Just what is a prodrome, Girandole, pray tell?"

"I must confess that—"

"They're quite done in, that is all. And monsieur must make the best of it. Here! Let him be the one to choose these galley oars. 'Tis his business. As for myself, I have seen what I needed to: we shall have barely forty men, and they shan't be in the pink."

The jollyboat, manned by Montpassé and his sailors, was no more than a black dot between the ship and the island. At six o'clock, after consulting the barometer and studying the clear sky one last time, Captain Bloche ordered the longboat slung over the ship's side. As they finished lowering away the heavy craft, he gave instructions that the two bosuns should pipe up all hands not necessary for the running of the ship.

Standing near the mainmast with Saint-Foin, as the shadows lengthened and the woodwork took on an orange glow, he watched a gray parade straggle by, weary and all dusty with the evening's powdery light. One would have thought these people truly condemned to the galleys. Knowing they could still avoid selection—and doing their utmost to achieve this end, or overdoing it—they presented Saint-Foin with a thorny problem. After all, most of them would have been excused under normal circumstances. This man was blind in one eye, that man limped, that other one had a nasty wound in the palm of his hand. Their sorry appearance was by no means make-believe: he saw bruised and pustular faces, cripples of all kinds, teeth missing in plenty, itching and oozing scabs, rheumy eyes, feet cut to shreds. The need to distinguish truth from falsehood came only when each beggar from this Court of Miracles launched into the recital of his ills, with all the moans and groans and revolting details necessary, in his opinion, for a faithful presentation of his case.

Bloche had hoped for forty men; Saint-Foin selected thirty-two. To these were added a topman found hiding in the hold and a sailor who had so expertly simulated extreme weakness that the surgeon had been fooled, until he chanced to see the invalid striding energetically away. Finally, they mobilized the two youngest of the five servants, personnel whom the bosuns had too scrupulously exempted from consideration. So, thirty-six men, whom Bloche divided into two watches that would each row for two hours.

The longboat shoved off at seven o'clock. The sun was sinking fast, and gauzy vapors filled the sky. Shortly afterward, the tow line grew taut and the oars, taking their pace from the regular cries of the bosun, Vallier, began their rhythmic sweep of the dark water.

For a long time, the ship did not budge, but sat in her basin like a castle in a moat. Then the filth floating at the waterline began, very slowly, to move. The mountain was languidly leaving its bed.

At nightfall, a slight lapping was finally heard. Far ahead, the oars labored. The monotonous dip of their blades measured out the silence like a clock.

III.

THE FOLLOWING DAY was lifeless. The rowers, who had relayed each other until eight o'clock that morning, slept suspended in their hammocks like a crowded colony of sweating fruit bats. Rank smells and ogreish sighs drifted through the ovenlike between-decks. Topside, a few men of the watch, weakened and idle, had stuck their heads into little patches of shadow and dozed off, scratching their sun-baked hams through their trousers. The wooden vessel crackled and creaked and snapped as though that huge mass of oak were being consumed by an invisible fire.

The island was hardly any closer at all. No one knew how many miles they had covered. They knew only that the ship was marinating once more in the smooth, heavy water that lay sleeping all the way to the horizon.

Five men had reported to the sick bay. Two were rowers who complained of aching joints and intense itching.

The Traveler's Tree

The other three were suffering, respectively, from a griping stomach pain, a carbuncle, and an ugly arm wound. Saint-Foin recognized these last as men he had exempted the previous day, for in addition to their ailments they demonstrated what he called "a manifest cachexia." He had them all bled, prescribed cream of tartar, squillitic wine, ointments, and vesicatories, and relieved the two oarsmen of their rowing duties, but he kept none of them in sick bay.

There were enough on the sick list as it was. A few of these had taken rapid turns for the worse, like the filthy man afflicted with the bloody flux. He had shriveled into what looked like a grotesque little black monkey, dying with a hateful rictus, his teeth bared by cracked, swollen lips. Saint-Foin returned to his bedside every hour with angry obstinacy. He sensed, within that horribly gaunt head, a kind of meanness that might be capable of fighting back. He was so sure of this that he considered discontinuing the laudanum in order, he thought, to give the patient a free hand. When the effects of the last dose wore off, however, he realized that the man had only enough strength left to moan.

Saint-Foin felt quite hot all afternoon and was twice overcome by the stench. Instead of growing used to it, he had violent attacks of nausea that drove him on deck for fresh air. He wondered how Robinot could appear unaffected, and thought, "That man must be numb in the nose."

At six o'clock, he visited Picot-Fleury. On the previous

day he had merely bled him and left him a small flask of peppermint-water. The vomiting had ceased. A hopeful sign, but the fever had not abated, and the patient was now racked by stabbing abdominal pains. Early that morning, too weak to rise from his bed in time, he had soiled himself with diarrhea.

Although the port was open and Dominique was emptying the chamber pot out the porthole promptly after each use, the odor in the cabin was sickening, and made even worse by the burning orris root that was meant to perfume the air. The already cramped space was further diminished by a cloth that had been hung to close off a section for Dominique. There was only enough room for a mattress laid upon a sideboard, a small bureau, a chair, and a chest. Most of the naturalist's baggage was stowed in the huge storage area on the main deck, with the baskets and cages.

Perspiration bedewed the patient's drawn face, his turned-up nose, his cheeks roughened by a blond stubble. With two fingers, he would pinch his loose, sweat-soaked shirt and puff it away from his body. Suffering in turn from chills and feverish heat, he kept drawing up and pushing back the bedclothes.

When the sick man uncovered a leg, Saint-Foin noticed some marks he had not expected to see. He questioned him. When had this rash appeared? Did his joints ache? Had he felt weak even before his illness?

Picot-Fleury answered him, then clutched at the surgeon's forearm.

"Am I infected as well?"

Saint-Foin reassured him: he was suffering from a kind of poisoning that had predisposed him to these symptoms, which would disappear as soon as they reached the island. The important thing was to tackle this intestinal disorder, to combat it with a suitable treatment. He would attend to that right away. "Dominique," he called, to prove his determination, "you will come to the dispensary for the preparation this evening."

"What vile antidote do you mean to give me?" asked Picot-Fleury.

"Two scruples of Turkey rhubarb and one scruple of powdered nutmeg. So you cannot very well say that I am torturing you!"

Saint-Foin stayed on. The patient seemed to relax; he had drunk some water scented with spirits of peppermint and chewed a bit of bread dipped in broth. He forgot his fever as he chatted, questioning Saint-Foin about the island, the weather, the distance they had covered.

Then he talked about his work and his role in the expedition, speaking with great modesty and a touch of humor. He did not know what might come of his two thick notebooks of observations. From his herbaria, his birdcages, his collecting cases, he wished to keep only one coleopter, two macaws, and one dicotyledonous plant belonging to the Nyctagineae. He acknowledged that he had been invited along on this voyage merely as an adjunct, and understood that his discoveries were valued no more highly than were the sketches and watercolors of the late, lamented Vuché de Beaune. The ambitions of this expedition had been far more grand. Most certainly! But then, of course, so had been its failure. And in the end, he found it amusing that the only tangible results of their mission, aside from a few drawings by Vuché, would be the fruits of his own labors.

His tone was almost playful. He was gently making fun of Trinquet when he broke off, grimacing with sudden pain.

"Pray excuse me," he said. "It would be better if you took your leave, at present."

"What is amiss?"

"I fear I should subject you to proceedings that are most unpleasant and quite malodorous."

Saint-Foin, in sudden comprehension, did not have to be asked twice.

"I am off. Take heart. The island is within reach. We shall be there inside of three days at the most."

"The island, yes, the island," said Picot-Fleury. Then his face became contorted with distress. "Go, Saint-Foin, I beg you!" he moaned. "Dominique, quickly, the bucket."

Saint-Foin vanished.

He felt he had had enough stench for one day. He went out on deck to breathe in the good salt air and the aroma of warm wood. He would have liked to think of nothing, or of very peaceful things. He contemplated the balusters, the handrails, the breastworks, the arcatures, the great shafts of the iron-bound masts—all that enormous wooden construction built to withstand the most violent knocking-about. He told himself that men should be made this ruggedly, for then they would need only a change of sails or some caulking here and there instead of falling apart in a thousand mysterious ways. What was poisoning Picot? Was it connected to the disease that was beginning to ravage him?

"…Cutaneous erethism, yes, but no ulceration. Constant sweating. His urine is clear, the gums red but not swollen. His torpor? Caused by this putrid fever and the exhaustion occasioned by diarrhea. We must flush out the humors. Allow the treatment to take effect…"

He remembered that he had to prepare his compounds.

"…Or else administer some ipecac, or an emetic based on tincture of myrrh. Elixir of vitriol? Come now, there's no need for that…"

The griping in his belly had returned. He winced. Now his intestinal distress was complicated by constipation, which unusual symptom—when all about him were suffering from excessive looseness—he found most preposterous and annoying. For a moment he wondered if his special status as surgeon guaranteed him special ailments. Perhaps he was safe from this rotting disease…

"Nonsense!" he told himself. "Truly, we are all in the same boat—aside from this capricious problem, for which I'd be well advised to try some senna tea."

His pain gradually subsided. Finally lost in idle reverie, he leaned his elbows on the rail and watched the sun go down. His eyes peered from between their doggish, wrinkled lids at the tiny bump on the horizon. As on the two previous evenings, a haze began to obscure the rosy sun sitting practically on top of the island, which almost appeared, in the fluid, swirling light, to be on fire.

One by one, as though drawn by the cooler air, sailors emerged from the depths. They seemed like peasants trudging to their daily labors in the fields. Saint-Foin noticed their lassitude, however, and saw in each man worrisome signs of infection. He turned away, and soon closed his eyes.

"Sleep," he thought. "Yes, to sleep, like Du Mouchet..."

He heard the bosun's whistle, shouted orders, foot-steps. The longboat thumped repeatedly against the side; there were cries, a hollow trampling aboard the boat, and then, at a crisp command, the splash of oars. Soon their slow, rhythmic rowing was heard, bearing off.

Lulled by a sound like the twirling of a weather vane from somewhere overhead, Saint-Foin neither moved nor opened his eyes for a long while. He did not feel the gentle motion of the *flûte*. It was only when he looked out over the rail again that he realized the ship was gliding through the water without a ripple.

The sun had set in its violet haze. The sea was only a dull gleam of pewter. Saint-Foin watched the sky darken over the water until there was no edge between them. Then he went to prepare the grilled rhubarb and powdered nutmeg before going in to supper.

*

During the night there occurred an event which they had no longer dared to expect: it rained. It was a light shower that passed as swiftly as it had come. Everyone felt refreshed, and began to hope. It was too much to ask. A great gust of wind had come right before the rain, but there had been no time to make sail, and immediately afterward the calm returned.

That morning, in the early light, the island had grown tolerably larger. Colinet was the first to observe her with his spyglass, through air still thick with fog. To the south rose a bluff cut by escarpments. A deeper indentation marked the rise of a second, higher bluff, separated at its summit into two humps. Then came a long slope, breaking at a kind of promontory and continuing beyond it to vanish into the ocean.

That was all he could see until dawn. When the morning mist had cleared, he observed the dark, lush coat covering all the heights except the promontory on the northern side, and he was able to make out tongues of tender green along the hills. The steep bluff to the south overlooked a chaos of reefs. Elsewhere appeared edgings of white sand, interrupted here and there by the overflowing vegetation.

Shortly afterward, Girandole made the same observations, followed by the two bosuns, and then Malestro. They examined the approaches to the island and the stretch of sea separating her from the ship, searching for Montpassé and the jollyboat. They found nothing.

Satisfied by the reports of his officers, Bloche had felt

no need to interrupt his breakfast to come see for himself. The island appeared bounteous; they need no longer fear a landfall on some arid, barren stone. And although Montpassé was nowhere to be seen, he might be sighted at any moment. It was too early for concern.

When the captain emerged, just before eight o'clock, he intended simply to look for a possible anchorage near the island. The deck was crowded with tired but happy men, and he passed among them without paying attention to the few impatient souls who spoke of sending out the longboat with her towline then and there. Up in the port bow, he took the spyglass handed to him by Colinet and studied the island's shores.

At that distance, details were limited to pastel smears and the snags of reefs, but the captain's expert eye, that big fishy eye, quickly discerned what the others had missed. He swept the glass across the island twice more, just to be sure, then returned it to Colinet.

"There are breakers from north to south," he observed gravely.

At the news, the men's euphoria died away. They had considered this possibility, but without taking it seriously: an island does not present herself to you so opportunely, only to rebuff you.

Throughout the morning, eyes strained to find a passage, but in vain. They were too far away, and the syrupy water broke upon the coral in only the thinnest chaplets of downy froth. After all, if there were no gap in this barrier, that would explain the absence of Montpassé, who

would be obliged to row some way around the island—
who knew how far?—in search of a passage.

Bloche had shut himself up, first within his cabin, then
inside the lavatory, where he had had buckets of seawater
poured over his back. During dinner, he explained that it
would be unwise, given the cruel toll on the men, to try
pulling the ship around either end of the island. They
would continue right ahead until they found an anchorage, by which time, he expected, Montpassé would have
returned from his reconnaissance.

The afternoon drifted by, punctuated by the report of
the gun the captain had ordered fired every two hours to
signal the jollyboat. At one point the barometer fell sharply, and the sky quickly grew leaden. Another squall seemed
imminent. The men waited for it, prepared this time to
catch its water and its wind, with all sails set. Their hopes
were dashed, however, when they received nothing more
than a few drops like those sprinkled by a laundress at her
ironing table. Blue shone through the tattered clouds. The
ship had enjoyed barely a moment of breeze. The winds
blew high overhead and would not come down.

Before seven o'clock, once the sun had slipped behind
the northern headland, the atmosphere thickened upon
the island. A gray mantle floated over the hills, gathering
in the crevices and fluttering before the escarpments. One
of these plumes was so distinct that some observers took it
for a wreath of smoke. The embarking longboat party and
a few hands on deck noticed it at the same time, and urged
Girandole to look through his spyglass. The first mate

searched the foliage for the source but detected nothing.

"It would have to be quite a large fire," he said.

No one listened to him. The trees might easily hide the flames. And confound it, smoke spreads out—with a bushelful of live coals you could eat up half the sky.

"We shall see come nightfall," said Girandole.

"Who knows if this fire will last till then?" they replied, already on the defensive against skeptics.

The longboat was pulling again. Darkness settled on the water. In the bows of the ship, near the port cathead, loomed the black silhouette of the captain, a Pharaonic figure at the prow of his colossal chariot. This evening, the hieratic and majestic progress of the convoy and its leader had clearly affected the men still on deck. They began spitting out their quids, standing tall at the rail, looking off toward their destination with that fixed and noble gaze of coach dogs perched on a carriage.

Toward midnight, the leadsman found bottom: sand and coral at one hundred and ten fathoms. Bloche let the ship glide on. Two hours later, they were at sixty fathoms. They advanced through the sooty dark, guided only by the longboat's lantern. The island was no more than a great starless void. Fleeting scents of leaves and humus wafted by on the warm air and were inhaled with devotion. No fire; no noise save that of the oars and the vague, distant rustle of the sea breaking on the coral. Beyond, the silence of a sleeping forest.

The rising moon was in the first quarter as livid streaks shot through the eastern sky. The ship's gun shattered the silence. The island, whose lofty outline could just be seen, sent back the echo and returned to her vast stillness. Now one could distinguish a subtle range of blue-grays on her flanks, but blurry patches began to appear, and at dawn, the haze closed in.

The convoy crossed a local current that carried the boat and then the ship slightly to starboard. At six o'clock, Bloche recalled the longboat and dropped a bower in twenty-five fathoms of water. Then everyone went off to their berths. They were anchored three cables' lengths from the reef. Land was two thirds of a mile away.

The isle awoke in a confused chirping of birds and insects. Fleecy woods carpeted the heights. Here and there were terraces covered with blond velvet or dappled with clumps of trees. Ravines coursed down the slopes, some opening onto cliffs, and from one of them, cut into the naked rock of the southern versant, cascaded a waterfall. At its foot and nearby could be seen small coves, with their crescents of sand. To the north they discovered two beaches crowned by windmilling coconut palms. And before this shore lay the pale green waters of the lagoon, enclosed by a border of curling white breakers.

Spyglasses scanned the island until noon, searching both for a passage and for Montpassé's boat. They found neither one of them.

*

Bloche was at dinner, lounging in his chair, his waistcoat unbuttoned and sweat dripping from every ringlet of his wig. He had listened to Saint-Foin and then Colinet. The surgeon had announced the admission of three more patients to the sick bay, and the subsequent necessity of pushing the bulkheads out still farther to accommodate them. The young third mate—alias Lieutenant Chicken Coop—had informed him that the flour barrels were so spoiled and infested that even the rats were turning up their noses.

Bloche gave him permission to jettison the barrels and asked if anyone else had a calamity to report. Then Trinquet spoke up.

After much entreaty, he had been persuaded to consult his books and maps.

"I thought of Valmate," he said, "and of that island he mentions, which others have tried in vain to find again. Clearly, Valmate's coordinates are incorrect. But we are in that stretch of the ocean, give or take a few hundred miles. After all, the description of it in his journal is very similar. I should not care to overstate the case. I will say only that if it is Valmate's island, then we, gentlemen, will be the first to confirm the existence of a place that until now was believed to be imaginary."

The others hastened to inquire if Valmate had landed on the island.

"No. He sighted it one evening and bore down upon it, but he did not have our good fortune. By first light, the isle had disappeared. Consequently, you will understand why his discovery was for a long time left in doubt."

"Very well, then!" exclaimed Bloche. "Now we know what we are dealing with."

"We must not be too hasty, Captain," protested Trinquet. "This is merely a hypothesis! A well-founded one, of course, but still, a hypothesis."

"Certainly, dear friend, we understand," said Bloche, for whom this question was no longer an item on the agenda.

Then, coming to a point he regarded as far more important, he considered the fate of Montpassé, without undue alarm, simply reviewing the possible explanations for his delay in returning to the ship. For in his opinion it was only a delay. What real dangers could the jollyboat have encountered? The weather had been calm, and the island, to all appearances, was uninhabited.

"And yet," noted Girandole, "some of the men thought they saw smoke from a fire yesterday evening."

This observation, albeit a cautious one, did not sit well with the captain.

"They thought they saw. Is that all? Men are always seeing things. Men have been seeing things for centuries. Half our charts must be credited to this gift of second sight. What would you have me do? Did you observe any dugout canoes? No. Any people? No. Then spare me such tales, if you please. There is no one on this island, I assure you. And this is precisely what worries me…"

He remained silent for some time, thus allowing his

listeners to ponder this contradiction: Was he afraid that there *were* people on the island, or that there were *not*? Finally, prompted by the chevalier, he explained his point.

"If there is no one, gentlemen, would it not be because it is impossible to set foot there?"

Once more he left the others to think over the implications.

"That is only a conjecture, Captain," offered Malestro at last. "And here is another one: suppose that someone has come and gone."

"Whatever for, Monsieur Malestro? To lay an egg there?"

"Captain," replied Girandole, "if the island were inaccessible, Montpassé would have already returned."

"Indeed," added Trinquet, "I think you go too fast. Have we not visited other uninhabited islands?"

"We have."

"Well, then, what do you make of that?"

"They were mere pebbles. And I grant you that people may well have come and gone from such isles as those. But fruitful places are not readily abandoned. This island is fertile. Indeed, she is an enchanting little thing. Savages would not have failed to settle here."

"Only if they happened upon her."

"Men have scoured the seven seas, Monsieur Trinquet. Wherever we may go, others have passed before us. There are no more undiscovered lands, except in the estimation of a few hydrographers."

"Monsieur Bloche," retorted Trinquet huffily, "I—"

"Captain," exclaimed Saint-Foin, cutting off the old man, "we are getting nowhere. If we must go around in a circle, let it not be around this table, for it will lead only to bilgewater. Let us reconnoiter this island, and without delay. That is the only way to settle the question."

Bloche did not answer. An enormous pout locked up his entire face. The chevalier spoke for him.

"You are forgetting Montpassé, Saint-Foin. Shouldn't we wait for him?"

"Wait, monsieur? Is this the time for waiting?"

"At least he will bring us some information. And 'tis perhaps only a question of a few hours."

"Or a few days. We have no idea what has happened to him. Who knows where he is now and in what difficulties he may be?"

Bloche broke his silence.

"You must not paint things blacker than they are, Saint-Foin."

"I have no need to, Captain. They are dark enough. And I should like you to appreciate this fact."

"But I do—great God! What will it take to convince you? Must I wipe every backside in your sick bay?"

"Do not wait for Montpassé."

Bloche made a gesture of irritation.

"As you wish, then! We will arm the longboat and send the galley slaves back to their oars. Are you satisfied?...Girandole, you shall be in command. You will leave as soon as possible, since our surgeon would have it so. But I require you to return by nightfall. You will load a swivel gun upon the longboat, to be fired once every hour. As for you, Saint-Foin, I forbid you to make even the slightest request of me until tomorrow!"

At three o'clock that afternoon, Girandole climbed down into the longboat. Waiting for him there were the bosun, Baudin, and twenty men chosen from among the most fit and resolute members of the crew. They carried some casks, weapons, water, and the swivel gun fixed to the prow. It had been decided that the detachment would work its way southward around the island, examining the approaches to the coves and skirting the reefs to explore the far shore.

The boat stood in toward the coral barrier. An hour later, it was in front of the coves and the waterfall.

Those on board ship soon saw a plume of smoke and then heard the report of the gun, which echoed off the bluff. The figure of the first mate, standing in the bow, could be seen through the spyglass. The rowers kept up a steady pace, as though there were no point in lingering before an impenetrable barrier.

Half an hour later, the longboat passed the outer edge of the reefs, first pulling well off to sea before turning back inland. It had rounded the southern spit of the island, meanwhile, and so was soon lost to view.

They waited. Toward five o'clock, the firing of the gun was heard faintly. It was at this point, if he had not found an opening, that Girandole was to swing around and return to the ship.

The air was appallingly humid and oppressive. Bloche stood on the port gangway mopping his pate with his wig, which he held balled up in one hand. He had given the spyglass back to Colinet and was studying the heavens. Whatever he saw there did not reassure him.

"I wager the barometer is taking a tumble," he said sharply. "I know this weather. 'Twould not surprise me if a few hundred miles from here a hurricane were up to its tricks."

Off to the east massed dingy thunderclouds tinged with bronze in the vast sweeps of pale sky. This poisonous, ponderous cloudbank was the only thing in motion. The sea was flattened, the air as thick as soup.

"A fine time for it," sighed Bloche. "Colinet, let go the sheet anchor." Glancing aloft, where the sails were snugly furled once more, he added, "What use is this wind to us now? It comes too late. Let it bring us some water, that is all I ask…'Twill perhaps be no more than a few drops, but who can say? Have tubs and buckets brought out."

At six o'clock, the swivel gun was heard again, this time more clearly. Ten minutes later, the longboat emerged from behind the reefs. Great dark billows began boiling overhead. All whiteness went to gray, and an opaque brown dust cloud, like something raised by galloping horses, was rapidly filling the sky. In another moment, the shadow swept down upon them. The brown dust had become muddy and black, and foul weather roiled over the entire sky. A shiver passed across the sea, followed by a huge gust of warm wind. A crackling had begun. It grew louder. It arrived in a rush with a wall of water.

The ship was submerged in the rattling torrent. It was impossible to see five feet ahead. A swarm of gray grasshoppers was splashing down everywhere. All around, everything glittered, clinked, splattered, crashed, and the wind would toss shovelfuls of hot pinpricks into the men's faces. No one had taken shelter, however. Standing motionless, they braved the onslaught. They welcomed the water as piously as if it were a baptism.

The shower was brief, and the downpour moved off to drench the slopes of the island. It left behind a fragrant vapor and scattered trickling sounds that made the entire *flûte* gurgle softly. It also left the sailors dazed but happy, softly licking their lips before rushing to plunge both hands into the buckets.

It was only then, refreshed, that they remembered those out on the water. Bloche was already looking for them with the glass. He saw nothing. Sheets of rain had just passed over the edge of the lagoon, leaving swirls of mist in their wake. When the last tail ends of wind finally dispersed them, the longboat appeared, still afloat, toiling along a stretch of coral reef.

"They weathered it," said Bloche. "All's well."

Colinet immediately passed on the news, and there were cries of joy from those on deck. Reassured, Bloche handed the glass to Colinet and attempted to wipe himself off. Fishing out his wig, which he had crammed into his pocket, he found it soaked. His handkerchief was not much better. Vexed, he wiped the back of his sleeve across his dripping nose and winkled his snuffbox from his waistcoat pocket. Colinet did not give him time to open it.

"Captain, I am not certain they are in such a fair way. Look."

Taking back the spyglass, the captain saw that there was indeed a commotion in the longboat. Although some oars were rowing, Girandole was no longer standing in the prow. He was definitely among those in movement amid the oarsmen. Bloche quickly sized up the situation.

"They're bailing," he said.

"The rainwater?"

"Don't be an ass! They have sprung a leak."

The boat was about two miles off, and as the last vapors melted away, it could be seen more clearly. It seemed hardly to advance, even though the crew labored valiantly at both pulling the oars and scooping out water.

"That gust of wind beat them back," said Bloche. "They must have struck upon a hidden rock...The boat is horrid heavy. Judging from their draft, they are not gaining any advantage."

The waterlogged craft proceeded sluggishly, taking forever to cover barely half a mile. Now Bloche could make out Girandole bailing with his hat, and Baudin tossing casks over the side. Both of them then tackled the swivel gun, which they managed to unshackle and heave overboard.

Although some of those nearby and lined up along the bulwark shouted encouragement, the captain could see that the longboat was almost gunwales under.

"They are done for," he said.

Despite all efforts, the longboat truly was sinking. They covered another few cables' lengths in the greatest agitation; then, all as one, the men stopped moving. They remained frozen in amazement for a good long moment while the boat settled into the water.

All had fallen silent on the ship. Shocked into action by the flood, those in the longboat began to scrabble about for empty barrels, masts, oars detached from their oarlocks—anything to float them back. Floundering in the swamping water, everyone tried to snag a buoy. Seen from the ship, the struggle was so confused, one could not tell if they were helping each other or fighting over pieces of wood.

A few men were observed striking out for the *flûte*; one by one, the others followed, until the entire flock was bobbing in the water. The sea was once again a perfect sapphire blue.

The first swimmers reached the ship only at nightfall. Survivors were counted as they arrived. No one was missing.

IV.

IT WAS ONLY WITH great reluctance that Saint-Foin had resigned himself to further expanding the area of the sick bay. He felt as though he were giving the disease room to grow and prosper with its tubercles, its ulcers, its swollen gums. He even wondered, watching his patients eat with gusto, if they were not feeding the illness as well, helping it to reduce them to the state of that dying man over there who had lost all appetite for anything. It was the grubby little man. He was finished. Each short breath rattled in his throat. A dribble of clotted blood ran down from his nose into the yellow spittle buttering his lips. His carrion stench was ghastly and impossible to dispel. Even with all ports open, the stink hung in the still and humid air, delighting the fat, excited flies.

When Saint-Foin went off to welcome the survivors from the longboat (if anyone went missing, he thought, at least he would be spared this suffering), he felt the little man was hanging by a thread. The surgeon feared his patient would be dead when he returned, but he was wrong. The man did not die until half past eleven.

The night was sweltry and stagnant. Unwilling to remain in their berths chewing hot cotton for air, the men had gathered on the warm planking of the deck in a bivouac without arms or baggage, their bodies lost in the shadows, which were alive with sighs, groans, and the murmur of someone telling his life's story. From the island came a distant and confused concert of flutes, phrased by the deep cries of birds, a melodious, soothing sound that lulled its listeners with something sweet and rapturous. The starry sky cleansed the soul. They listened to the void. They even forgot the sea, so quiet was the water, black and heavy as tar. Sleep would not come: this vast nocturnal calm bewildered them.

At midnight, some men brought up the canvas-shrouded corpse and placed it by the mainmast. Even though everyone moved away, then farther and still farther away, it was not enough: the miasmal smell was inescapable. In the end, the sailmaker Guyader went bravely off to awaken the captain so that the funeral service could be held without delay. Bloche understood. He soon appeared, treading loudly, with his particular way of throwing his legs forward as he walked. With the exception of his waistcoat, at which he had balked, he was completely rigged out, but only half buttoned up, and he seemed twice as large as he did in broad daylight. Although the men expected crabbiness, he was surprisingly gracious.

"Come on, lads!" he said, reaching the mainmast. "No need to keep this poor boy waiting."

The cook's plank was ready. The ceremony was performed with a few words and a doffing of hats; the body, duly weighted, sank into the tar. When it was over, the crew went off to lie down upon the deck again, carefully avoiding the place where the corpse had lain, however, for in spite of all the water and vinegar they threw upon it, they could not wash away the stink.

Besides, they did not like to bury their dead from a ship at anchor, especially with less than twenty-five fathoms beneath the keel. Crabs have a taste for drowned flesh, and if they get to work on the seams, then up pops the cadaver, half eaten, with empty eye sockets, the mouth teeming with tiny creatures feasting away— unless a shark has been chewing at the hams and guts...

The crew were not alone in suffering from the stifling atmosphere. It was equally oppressive in the small cabins below the quarterdeck and in those beneath them where the assistants, servants, and petty officers were lodged. Every now and then during the night, someone would come topside for an hour or two in search of air. Guyader, the chief carpenter Le Cam, the chief gunner Lesur, and Baudin, the bosun who had swum to safety from the longboat, had all decided to spend the rest of the night in the open, stretched out on deck among their men.

Many had finally fallen asleep when the chevalier emerged from his quarters.

This visit was most unusual, for the men rarely saw

the chevalier. He hardly ever set foot outside his cabin and had not so much as stood leaning on the taffrail for some weeks. Those who watched him now speculated that his cabin, with all its ports wide open, must have been hot indeed to drive him from his gilt bed and white linen sheets. And he was said to sleep soundly—absolutely like a log! At sea, anyway. The sea had that effect on him. As soon as he reached land, he was another man. He left the ship to rove about like a bitch in heat—or rather, like a lion on the prowl. At the approach of an island, he'd start stretching his limbs. You'd have said he could smell land, that bugger. Mind you, all that was yesterday. This time he'd not bestirred himself at all. What was more, no one had seen hide or hair of him. As though he didn't give a damn for this island here. Well and good! Only, why had he left his lair, then? Perhaps the pretty thing had gotten under his skin just a bit after all?

Du Mouchet had silently crossed the quarterdeck, weaving his way through the sleeping figures. He was bareheaded, wearing only his shirt and breeches. He might have been taken for one of the hands, had it not been for his boots and the honey-pepper aroma his cigar left in his wake.

He was surprised and certainly irritated to find so many people underfoot. When he reached the mainmast, he searched in the gleam of the lanterns for a less crowded spot. He decided to climb to the maintop. Approaching the shrouds, he was reaching for the hawser-laid rope when someone spoke.

"Useless, monsieur."

Malestro was on the gangway, about five feet from him.

"Some topmen have already gone up, and there is no more room."

Malestro was leaning back against the bulwark, glass in hand; his voice was deep and even. He, too, was in shirtsleeves and boots.

"If you wish to smoke up there in peace, you will be obliged to dislodge them. They will obey, but most unwillingly, I promise you. The place is much sought after, as it affords the only faint current of air to be found tonight anywhere on the *Entremetteuse*...aside from your quarters, perhaps."

The chevalier abandoned his plan and walked slowly along the gangway.

"You are much mistaken," he replied. "The atmosphere in my rooms is also uncommon close, but I can make the best of it. I was asleep. A bad dream awakened me."

Malestro watched the chevalier approach; his glass smelled of rum.

"As you can see, this spot is not taken. The gangway is too narrow for anyone to stretch out upon in comfort."

"True," said the chevalier simply, leaning back against the bulwark next to the other man.

They were silent for a moment. From the waist below rose the sighs of heavy sleep and the smells of tar, wood, and mildew. They heard the myriad flutes of the island in the distance; closer by, the sea broke in whispers on the coral reef.

The party in the longboat had come up against this barrier—and then worked their way along a shore so steep-to that it was inapproachable. They would have explored farther, but there had not been enough time. And now, they could only speculate about their chances...

A few of the men, including Malestro, harbored a secret reproach they had not dared utter before the captain: he should have let the reconnaissance party press on, without requiring their return by nightfall.

"I do fear," said Malestro, "that we have missed our opportunity to get a foothold. He ought to have let Girandole go on."

The chevalier took his time before answering.

"It was a prudent decision," he said. "Pointless to regret it. We will await Montpassé, that is all."

With these last words, he looked meaningfully at Malestro. Although his person exhibited that sort of lassitude common to heavy sleepers and debauchees, his eyes always gleamed with vitality.

"It would seem, monsieur," ventured Malestro, "that you have no great desire to conquer this island."

"What would I do with her?"

"Ah, well...Whatever you did with the others."

"In that case I should have to discern some new mysteries in her, but I have lost the innocence and ignorance this game requires."

"Lord! You are blasé indeed."

"Well, let us say I no longer feel the attraction of these little worlds. You see, their illusion has gone the way of my innocence. I know only too well that distressing moment when one realizes one has seen everything there is to see."

Musing in the blue smoke of his cigar, he thought over what he had just said. Was it really a question of innocence? Had he been innocent when the first islands had offered themselves to him? Perhaps he had simply felt a splendid passion and a deep wonderment, believing, with some reason, that they held the answer to many of his desires.

"But what about you, Malestro?" he continued. "Does this island interest you, then?"

"Perhaps."

The chevalier began to laugh softly.

"You are incorrigible. Here we are in desperate straits, and you show more care for your private affairs than for your very life. So you think yourself immortal?"

"No, monsieur, but I am not dead yet. While my life is in your hands, let me still look to my future."

The chevalier smiled. Then he took one final puff on his cigar and tossed it overboard. Malestro drank the last drops of rum in his glass. Both of them gave in to the vague melancholy aroused by that sultry night.

A long while passed before the chevalier spoke again.

"This message, then, that has sent you scurrying around on all our islands—it still has some value?"

"What message, monsieur?"

"Come, come, Malestro. You know perfectly well that we are aware of your doings. Your mysterious expeditions, your surveying instruments and digging tools, your questioning of the natives. And that sudden dash for the ship with those savages at your heels…But tell me, what did happen that day? Oh, I know, you gave your explanation. Your lies did not persuade a single one of us. What was the truth of the matter?"

"It was a misunderstanding."

"But what happened?"

"I was on the wrong tack: a word, one simple word, misunderstood."

"A word in the message?"

It was Malestro's turn to smile, with lips that parted grudgingly and refused to reveal his teeth. Yesterday, he had been prepared to carry his secret with him to the grave. Today, tonight, it seemed less precious to him. What was this message worth now? He could see the old paper, the clumsy handwriting, the bottle in which he had kept it, curiously enough. Of what use to him was that miserable bottle hidden under his mattress? Out of spiteful vexation, but knowing also that Du Mouchet would never seek to compete with him, Malestro nodded.

"So this message is quite obscure," said the chevalier.

"Less so than others."

"You are said to possess a collection of them."

"Oh, a few, in Caine."

"What do they say?"

"For the most part, they are devoid of interest. Often they are nothing more than cries for help."

"You say that with such cynicism!"

"Do you think, monsieur, that a few words dashed off on a scrap of paper would suffice to raise an expedition? To search for some poor devils lost in the middle of the ocean and perhaps already reduced to sun-bleached bones?"

"All right! And the others?"

"Relics of notes written by famous hands and messages so well coded that they are indecipherable."

"The one that interests you now, is it in code?"

"No. But, forgive me, you would make nothing of it. It mentions a Ravenala, a monkey..."

"At least let me hear the whole thing."

Malestro was in a confiding mood. He glanced around to make sure that no one else was within earshot.

"On Joachim's isle. Ravenala on the monkey's shoulder. Thirty paces straight from his open hand."

"So that is the enigma that has so preoccupied you since our departure...Joachim's isle, you say? No one has ever spoken of it."

"There is no known place of that name. Of all the seamen named Joachim, a few have discovered islands, but without naming them after themselves. Those have run me a merry race. Several times I thought I had found my quarry."

"So did I," said the chevalier. "What were you looking for? A clutch of eggs left by some hen?"

"I think I hear the captain speaking."

"Gold, am I right?"

"Who does not search for gold?"

"Well, it seems that you have lost the game, Malestro. Like the rest of us."

"Perhaps, monsieur."

"What do you mean, 'perhaps'? Still being secretive, I see."

"Oh, not so very."

"Explain yourself."

"According to Trinquet, this island was discovered by Valmate."

"So it would seem."

"Others have since searched for it on the strength of his account. In vain. The island is credited to him all the more surely in that he alone has vouched for its existence."

"You amuse me, Malestro. Here you are, caught up in the chase once again. Go on."

"The Valmate we speak of is Joachim de Valmate…"

Suddenly they heard a frightful whinnying in the sick bay below. They stopped talking to listen. Some men in the waist had also held their breath and pricked up their ears. The voice was exceedingly high and shrill, and sounded like the shrieking of a madwoman.

Shortly afterward, they saw Robinot come out hurriedly and convince three men to go back inside with him. The cries continued for a few moments, then ceased abruptly.

The chevalier and Malestro did not resume their conversation. They waited, listening to the stubborn murmur of the breakers and the distant warbling of the island. It was not long before the three men returned to their places to lie down and began telling their neighbors what had happened. The chevalier questioned them from up on the gangway.

The disturbance behind this little incident had begun an hour earlier, when a patient had started to moan. Softly, at first, like a child whimpering, like a dog whining; then a brutish, insistent rhythm had emerged. Gasps and guttural shouts were added to this singsong. The man was lying motionless on his cot, but when Robinot came to give him some laudanum, all at once he began to thrash violently about, making those whinnying noises they had heard up on deck. A melee ensued when a few patients tried to help Robinot deal with the hysterical patient. After cursing vigorously, the surgeon's aide had rushed off to find assistance, returning with Lesur and two gunners.

The problem was then swiftly resolved. Lesur was compact and brawny. After asking his two companions to restrain the wild man's limbs, he grabbed the patient's hair, pulled his head up to the right height, and dealt him a bone-cracking blow to the jaw that made his swollen black gums bleed. One punch was all it took. The struggling man fell suddenly limp, while blood bubbled from his mouth. Lesur had not let go of his hair, so that he seemed to be grasping a severed head in his fist. He lowered it as gently as possible, as though fearing to awaken the man. When he loosened his grip, a great tuft of red hair, as brittle as burnt grass, came away on his fingers.

*

When the next day dawned on the same dead calm, Bloche sank into a foul humor. First he took out his irritation on his servant; then he took the proper steps to keep his men busy. And he began by ordering a fumigation of the between-decks and the hold.

The hands had expected to lie about in fretful idleness, instead of which it was all whistles, orders, and bustle. Having no faith in the efficacy of the operation, they did not fail to grouse about it. The disturbance was hateful. That cloying odor of urine, stale sweat, and rancid cheese belonged to them by now. Not only had they grown used to it, they clung to it. A way of marking their territory. Besides, they said, animals do the same thing: wherever they wish to stake a claim, they take a piss. These men would have found the counterpart to their scent in the pungent, acrid fumes of rabbit burrows, in the delicate decomposition of little birds' nests, in a jackal's stinking boneheap with its slobbery scraps of feathers and fur, in the musky wallow of wild boars, in the nauseous smell of a clutch of snake or tortoise eggs, in the pestilential slime and excrement of dogfish, in hills of guano that reek strongly enough to be scented long before they are sighted. The lower-deck stink reassured the men: it was theirs, their very own. It lived in their lair. The rougher such places are, the more of themselves men must put into them.

When everyone had been evacuated, all the ports, hatchways, and scuttles were closed. Colinet and Vallier, the bosun, had prepared the fumigant: a mixture of tar, juniper, gunpowder, and vinegar, poured into caldrons and set alight down in the hold.

Assembled on deck, the hands cursed this fumigation, insisting that the rats, flies, cockroaches, and fleas would come through it with flying colors, while the only thing left poisoned would be the crew's own air. As time passed, they grew restless and sought to amuse themselves. They soon found a way.

With all the exits closed, some rats nosing around topside were unable to return to the labyrinth below. They quickly became disoriented, nervous, imprudent. Once they were discovered, the chase was on.

At first, the most dim-witted specimens trotted between the men's legs, fatally close to death-dealing sandals and clogs. Then others stirred in the shadows of the gun carriages or inside coils of rope. They were soon flushed out and pursued with great uproar along the bulwarks. The crew had armed themselves with ax handles, mallets, and belaying pins, and they shouted like beaters at a hunt. Yet despite their panic, the rats did not give up so easily. The terrain belonged as much to them as it did to the men, for they were masters of its subtlest features and knew how to dart here and there, scooting along with disdainful assurance. They dodged blows, swerved abruptly, volt-faced, leaped over obstacles, and fled into deck-jumble and its shadows.

A few tried to escape by climbing up the shrouds. A bad idea: assassins awaited them in the tops. By the time the rats realized their mistake, it was too late: their retreat was cut off. Then they would hesitate, wavering, for the first and only time, but still flaunting their proud defiance. They would consider the planking, the water, and then jump...

The last ones ran out in the open and straight into ambushes. They received no second chances. Bastinadoes shattered their spines. The crumpled corpses uncurled slowly, like sponges soaking up water.

The men beat the ship for game from stem to stern. They gathered in groups, striking all together with their cudgels as though threshing grain. Others ran along the bulwarks, clubbing at each step, urging one another on with shouts and oaths. Armed with an iron spit, the cook waved his arms about and thrust home, elbows flapping. A young sailor who had just triumphed over a cunning adversary held this good-sized rat by the tail, showing his bloody snout to all and sundry. After capturing his prey in his cap, another seaman finished him off with a twist of his fingers.

Eventually, the game grew scarce, with only a few hunters left doggedly pursuing the wiliest survivors. Most of the crew then turned to making fun of those still trying to finish the job, who were swearing a blue streak. The last rat was killed by the cook. As he brandished his victim on the point of his spit, with his mustache bristling and his turban knocked down over one eye, a cheer rent the air.

The men tallied up the bag, then tossed everything into the sea, congratulating themselves on a *tableau de chasse* that would never be equaled by that damnable fumigation.

The men had eaten their dinner beneath a blazing sun. Stretched out on the deck, they puffed at their pipes, digesting their unappetizing fare. They sweated, scratched their scabby hides, ran black fingernails over a week's growth of beard or through their lousy hair. They laughed and shouted, chatting about the rat hunt.

Near the foremast, Le Cam, the master carpenter, lay flat on his back, listening to their comments without joining in. The chase had tired him; besides the pain in his gums and joints, there was a distressing buzzing in his ears.

Gazing aloft with his arms folded behind his head, he was the only person to see a rat coming down a shroud. The lone survivor of the massacre was two toises above the deck, descending carefully on the far side of the rope. All Le Cam could see was its paws and tail. His first thought was to alert his companions, but as he watched the rat's descent, he realized it would soon be within his reach, so he decided to take care of it himself. All he needed was a weapon. He spotted a swab handle next to one of his neighbors. It was precisely what he wanted. He could grab it at the right moment. He was ready. He waited.

Knowing that it would be dangerously exposed just before reaching the safety of the hammock netting, the rat came down the heavy rope with the utmost caution, but Le Cam could still clearly see its constantly twitching pink tail and the tiny claws gripping the hempen shroud. The rodent took forever to descend to a man's eye level, and then the carpenter thought it ripe for the plucking. He leaped to his feet. But his outstretched hand did not take up the stick. He felt a muffled thundering in his ears and a red explosion in his chest and skull. He stood there for moment, gaping. Then, as though all his bones had melted, he collapsed like a sack ripped open at the bottom.

The man's death saved the rat's life.

Chapter

V.

'TIS USELESS TO WAIT for the jollyboat," said the man leaning back against a gun in the waist. "They're two days overdue. They've been gone long enough to go round this pebble three times now. I'm telling you, they're done for."

He was stout and rosy-complexioned. He wore a singlet, trousers, and sandals dusted with flour. The two tanned, bare-chested men in front of him sat on a chicken coop, smoking their pipes without looking up at their companion.

"Why d'you say they're dead?" asked one of them calmly.

"Why haven't they returned?"

"How would I know?"

"There you are. Oughtn't to have been no hindrance in their way. Once or twice round this island would show there's no passage, and nothing for it but to stand out to sea and pull for the ship. You couldn't call that difficult."

"Who says there's no passage?"

"If there is one and they've found it, can you tell me what's become of them? Seen them, have you? Heard any gunshots? We're nose to bunghole with this island, so they'd hardly miss us. No! Any way you look at her, this island means trouble."

"You'd rather croak in your own shit? Poor bastard. She's as lovely as a garden, this island. I can smell her fresh water and mangoes from here."

"Bastard yourself, with your silly tongue hanging out, like that fox in the fable. How're you going to get to them, these mangoes of yours?"

"Haven't we never seen a reef before?"

"We have."

"We've even had to stand out to sea again for a night, not so?"

"We have."

"And in the end we found our anchorage."

"Well now, not always. And anyway, we'd boats, and some wind. We've none of that now. We're helpless as babes on a wormy old barky, and her in a pretty fix."

"Winds come up again."

"Aye, and when they do, we'd best head for open sea."

"Frichoux, you clot-head! Go back to your baking and leave us in peace."

"My baking! What baking might that be, pray? I've no more flour."

"So that's why you've turned to thinking. And made a botch of it…"

They saw the captain coming from the bows in the

company of the Chevalier Du Mouchet, Malestro, and Colinet. It was half past nine o'clock. They were astonished to see the chevalier up and about so early. There was no doubt about it: the commander had lately made quite a show of energy.

As the group approached, Frichoux doffed his cap and spoke to Bloche.

"Captain! Saving your presence."

Bloche was wearing his bulldog face. It was a bad time to bother him. He stopped, however.

"What is it?"

"The lads and me, we'd like to know what you've in mind to do now we're in a tight spot, so to speak."

"What do you mean?"

"Well, if we can't get through—"

"Who says we cannot get through?"

"You've a way, Captain?"

"Of course."

"Hell and death, Captain! How will you get us onto dry land?"

"I shall not get you there; you shall go there on your own."

"How's that?"

"You must sink or swim."

"But all our boats is gone."

"I said swim, you brute! With your arms."

Frichoux was taken aback. Then he began to laugh derisively.

"Ha, ha! That's a good one, Captain, that is! With them coral rocks, thank you kindly. They'd make mincemeat of us. And besides, there's barely three or four of the lads as knows how to swim in that fashion."

"So much the worse for you," replied Bloche, who went on his way.

He and his companions had just been to the sick bay, a visit intended to show the surgeon that his deep concern was being taken seriously. Saint-Foin had had no need to exaggerate his misgivings; the stench and spectacle had been enough. The surgeon had admitted four more patients, moving the bulkheads beyond the foremast. Soon they would run out of cots and space. If they did not land on the island soon, those who fell ill would have to be left lying in their hammocks.

After their visit, the men had decided to take some fresh air before inspecting the storerooms. Instead of going down the nearest ladder, at the entrance to the waist, they had walked aft along the main deck. Leaving the baker and two sailors behind, they stepped beneath the quarterdeck, and once past the mainmast, made their way down the next ladder they came to.

They continued past the between-decks companion-way—small cabins on either side reached aft to the gunner's storeroom; forward stretched the long, low, dark forest of stanchions and masts where the crew slung their hammocks—and descended into the enormous rib cage of the ship. At the sound of their boots, a steward's mate with a lantern had come to meet them at the foot of the second flight. He now led the group through a door to inspect the ship's provisions of biscuit and beans, stowed in storerooms above the powder magazine and half underneath the gunner's storeroom. Without the lantern, they would have been plunged in darkness, like the rest of the hold; only the powder magazine was illuminated, dimly, by a light that burned directly above a bucket of water.

In the bread room, another lantern was waiting for them, brought by Maringot, the ship's steward, who was standing before some open barrels. He seemed struck with dismay.

Bloche and his companions were soon dismayed as well when they discovered the state of the biscuit. Much of it was spoiled. As hard and dry as wood, these square little crackers that served as bread for the crew had grown moldy and now stank of boiled leather and soap. As Maringot broached other barrels, the men saw the reserve they had counted on dwindle away. Bloche tasted a bit, grimaced, and went no farther. The rest was undoubtedly in a similar condition. He instructed the steward to have his men open all the barrels, sort through the biscuit, and rebake in the oven any that might still be saved.

They left the mate to begin this task and went next door to check the vegetables. This time, they knew what to expect. The stores of cabbage and peas had been exhausted, and the rice eaten by rats. There remained only some tough-skinned, wormy kidney beans with the acrid taste of horse chestnuts, a bitter flavor that triumphed over any amount of oil and vinegar.

"The only wholesome things I see in all these barrels," observed Bloche, "are the worms."

He casually brushed off a cockroach that was climbing up his sleeve and wiped his perspiring face. Then he left the room and its tarry air, thick with the musty odors of swamp water and leeks and the resinous scent of pitch-smeared wood.

They retraced their steps. The lantern's halo set their shadows dancing along the passage. All this black wood sweated, leaving a pungent smell on the fingers when touched.

Maringot led the way into the room containing the provisions for the ship's staff, through which Bloche proceeded without pausing. The contents of his own plate had told him all he needed to know about the condition of these stores. The little they could see of the room in the pale, flickering light seemed promising, even though there were no hams hanging in the gentlemen's pantry, no jars of fat, no dried fruits. In reality, however, many of those barrels were empty, and the contents of the rest had gone bad. Only the wine from Caine, in its sealed bottles, continued to age well.

They heard a muffled scampering that paused, resumed, and was then followed by a faint tapping. Bloche halted.

"Colinet, did you fumigate in here?"

"Of course, Captain."

"Then your fumigation is worthless. Unless the rat I just heard is fresh from a stay in the country. But now that I think on it, was it not a cockroach that crawled upon my coat a few minutes ago?"

"I cannot say, Captain."

"It was indeed," remarked the chevalier, who until now had merely taken stock in growing vexation of the deplorable state of his vast larder.

"Good God Almighty!" shouted Bloche. "These vermin are tenacious of life. No man could have lasted an hour in that fug. And the mosquitoes, Maringot, are they gone?"

"No more than the flies or the gnats, Captain. However, of the three cats we had left, one has been done for, while another is in a bad way."

"Why did you leave them down here?"

"'Twas impossible to catch them…"

The men continued their inspection. In addition to the passages, ladders and galleries that ran along the side of the ship provided paths through the maze. It was easy to become lost there, and without a lantern a man might have thought himself swallowed up in a network of mine tunnels. These bottlenecks with their wooden bulkheads running beneath the low-hanging deck beams were constantly creaking and grating, so that any visitor soon felt as though he were trapped underground.

There were small rooms containing blocks, cordage, round shot, or perhaps only a scattering of straw, but all smelled strongly of mold and pitch; larger areas served to store water, firewood, spare sails and spars, cables, and other supplies.

The group had arrived, via a gallery amidships, in one of those large rooms, where the wine, flour, and salt provisions were stowed. Two steward's mates were there, shiny with sweat. Their lantern illuminated scores of barrels set on their sides and in piles, stowed snugly against the bulkheads. Lying about were ladders and the ropes that served, when slung over deck beams, to maneuver the largest casks, as well as mallets, wedges, and wooden buckets. There was a mixture of sharp odors here: vinegar, tar, wet wood, greasy wool, and the carrion reek of a slaughterhouse. Swarms of midges hung in the air.

The flour barrels had been set aside for disposal, but Colinet explained that he did not dare throw them overboard while the ship was at anchor. Bloche nodded his approval. He had one of the mates open a cask of salt meat, only to find it had become a kind of custardy slop resembling rice gruel. Everything he inspected next was swimming in the same sludge: the salt pork, beef, cod, herring. The stench of rotten fish overpowered all else, as though it were the acme of decay. By comparison, the cheese, now dry and robbed of its venom, smelled as harmless as dead flowers.

Bloche went next door into another large storeroom. Since his last inspection, two weeks before, their provisions had deteriorated more seriously than he had expected.

"This grub has turned to garbage," he said. "Not even vultures would touch it. This lot must all be sorted through, Maringot, if that is still possible. The unwholesome spoils what is yet edible and will end by poisoning us. I am prepared to reduce rations. I prefer that the men suffer from hunger rather than from rotten bowels."

Although the crew were threatened with hunger, they

were already tormented by thirst. Their water had been rationed all along, and now it had become foul. They had plunged red-hot irons or heated rocks into the storage casks, and disinfected the contents with vinegar or fumes of sulphur, but in vain. The water had acquired a pinkish-brown tinge, a revolting brackish taste, and an infestation of white worms that the men dreaded finding in their mugs.

Nevertheless, each man drank three pints of this water daily. At that rate, their supply would be exhausted in a week. One mile off was a watering place where they might fill every cask with fresh water. The cascade's misty plume could be seen from the ship. But how long would it take to reach it? Bloche himself did not know. After inspecting their reserves, he prudently decided to cut the water ration.

The group went no farther. Beyond lay only the lions' den, where the enormous cable of the sheet anchor was coiled down, and other storerooms housing cordage, sailcloth, firewood, and shot. They returned topside, emerging from the hatchway in the waist, in front of the galley. There they parted. Bloche and Malestro strode off to the great cabin, while Colinet and Maringot, after receiving their orders, returned to the storerooms. The chevalier remained in the open air to refresh himself after the sickening reek of the hold.

A few men lounged about, already fatigued from the heat. Seawater had been dashed on the deck; the odor of old wood hovered in the rising vapor. The cook had lighted his oven; the logs crackled. From the fireplace, which opened onto the forecastle planking, a pale stream of smoke floated straight up into the brilliant sky. The chevalier watched it disappear, then turned around to gaze at the maintop. Once again, he considered climbing up there to enjoy that little breeze everyone spoke of, and to admire—why not?—the much-praised attractions of the island. Then his attention was drawn by the sound of splashing and raised voices.

Stepping up onto the gangway, he leaned over the rail. The cabin boy was in the water. A line hanging from a between-decks scuttle was attached to his belt. He was clinging to a keg, using it as a buoy, and clumsily kicking his legs. Du Mouchet heard sailors calling out below.

"Look alive, boy, you're bobbing around like a cork."

"At this rate, you'll miss your supper, sure."

"Him, aye, but not the sharks."

The men whooped with laughter.

"They do like a lad's tenderest parts—sniff 'em out, they can. They'll come from twenty leagues around for such a dainty treat."

There was more laughter and jesting.

"Leave him to his paddling," said someone halfheart-edly. "You're spoiling the test."

"What of it? Look at him, he's getting nowhere. Like it or not—he won't make it."

"He did the bulk of it: he went in. You'd not of risked your hide that way, Ramberge."

"Listen, mate, Ramberge is not one for trying to swim,

and besides he don't splash about in muck. Just look at that water—a toad hole, it is."

"All the more reason not to mock the lad. He wagered he'd do it, and he did. Now 'tis but a question of time."

"True enough. Let's all meet here again tomorrow."

The boy struggled along with his keg, straining anxiously to keep his head above water as he made for the cleats set into the hull directly below the gangport. Although his inexpert thrashing made him roll from side to side with each kick, churning up the filthy water around the ship, he was very slowly approaching his goal.

Then the chevalier heard a harsh, cracked voice call out, "D'you see that fin coming on out there?"

Another man immediately joined in.

"Looks to me as there's two of them sharks. They've smelled fresh meat."

Du Mouchet looked out over the water. He saw nothing. The men, however, confirmed the approach of fins and urged the boy to top speed. Despite only half believing them, the swimmer thought it best to hurry. Amid all the shouting, he did not hear someone call out that he had nothing to fear. His movements grew more desperate and awkward.

Suddenly, he lost his grip on the keg. He swallowed a mouthful, coughed, and flailed his arms.

"That's enough! Haul him in!" cried a voice.

"Not yet!" came the reply.

The boy floundered like a dog. He panted and spat, sinking into that oily water as though weighted down by cannonballs. He grew panicky, and his splashing pushed the keg farther away.

"Haul in the line, I tell you!"

"What for? By the time he's brought in, he'll have drunk the sea and all its little fishies."

"Someone go get him from the gangport!"

The boy was indeed only ten feet from the ladder cleats. He had given up on the keg and was now trying to reach safety by threshing his arms.

Du Mouchet went to help him. Approaching the gangport, he spotted a coil of rope, one end of which he tossed to the boy, who caught hold of it. The chevalier stepped through the gangport, climbed down, and held out his hand.

"Gently, gently," he said, pulling the boy over to the ship. Grasping him by the waist, he helped him up the ladder. He had to hold him tightly to control his shaking. Beneath the rough skin of the boy's scrawny body, the chevalier could feel tubercles shifting over the bones. Repelled, he moved his fingers, only to encounter other nodules.

Up on the gangway, the boy immediately collapsed and sat coughing and gasping for breath. A long lock of stiff, blond hair hung over his nose, but he made no attempt to brush it aside. A silver medal trembled on his breast. The chevalier could plainly see the tiny pink tumors, as well as the yellowish spots on his legs. The boy's colorless lips parted, revealing the purple swellings on his gums. Overwhelmed with disgust, Du Mouchet stepped aside.

When two men ran up, he said simply, "Take him to Saint-Foin."

*

They led the boy off. The chevalier had turned away. Now he wanted more than ever to climb to the maintop. His clothes were wet in places, and he felt as though they had absorbed not simply water but humors from the boy's body as well.

He hauled himself up by the ratlines and through the lubber's hole to climb out on the top, which rode about five toises above the deck. He was alone. The platform, which had no guard rail, was quite spacious, and the view was much grander at that height. His enjoyment of this picturesque perch was enhanced by the furled sails and calm weather.

But the air was no better aloft. Even on the top, the atmosphere was unpleasantly thick and sticky like molasses. Below, the water was so smooth that the ship seemed to lie on marble. In the distance, the sparkling sunlight created a host of candle flames on a lattice-work sea. To the south he saw some frigates, then some smaller white birds that were fishing, skimming over the waves, where they would suddenly seem to strike sparks. Closer to shore, over by the reefs, other birds flitted about like a swarm of flies. Their squawking was so loud it could be heard on the ship. Beyond lay the vast ocean and the clean line of the horizon.

"An empty vastness," thought the chevalier. "Neither one road nor a thousand. Nowhere to settle down, or even to camp. A simple emptiness to be crossed, from one land to another, as one steps from stone to stone across a river.

This emptiness, and then the land, long awaited, longed for... Yes, a bit of land around a tree—like this top encircling its mast. The tiniest islet is worth more than all the ocean. Desire grows keener as one sickens of this watery desert, and the appearance of an oasis releases floods of emotion."

He remembered this slow crushing by the void. After his first few weeks at sea, he had already been much affected, finding relief only in sleep. He was primed. He had fallen madly in love with the first island.

They had landed on a green evening washed by showers. It was only a sweet little nipple that spread out into beaches, notched by a cove protecting an islet. The sandy shore was thickly set with palms. In the longboat, he had felt something devilishly like desire. This small world promised unknown charms; its breath seemed to caress him. The songs of the birds, the scattered sparkling of the leaves shedding their raindrops, the steely reflections on the dense foliage, the soft shadows stained by red explosions of flowers—all that radiant exuberance had won his heart. At that moment, he would have sworn he was entering Eden, never to leave it again...

From the maintop, he could see the entire length of the island, north to south. He knew those palm-clad hills. He had plunged boldly into them, armed only with his sword. He had visited deep, narrow valleys, so dark and sweltering; he had wound through ravines, climbed along bluffs, made his way through tangles of vines and across slippery stones, with his blade gliding before him like a snake. Yes, he had foraged a great deal in those fragrant, humid depths, but he had also loved the clearings by the shoulders of hills, carpeted with downy grass and crowned with short palm trees that chattered softly in the slightest sighing of the wind. These were splendid moments of happiness, yet at length they were effaced— not by lassitude or boredom, but by an insidious sense of enclosure. Gradually, the fear of reaching the limits of this enclosure would become an obsession with him, spoiling his pleasure. Then he would flee.

Did this island hold the same fate in store for him? Without a doubt. And it was useless, he thought, to seek promises of eternal enchantment in his contemplation of the island. Of all those he had known, he recalled only two or three with any longing. And after all, he was under no illusions: he only regretted having left them before exhausting all their pleasures...

The sun was directly overhead, beating down on his shoulders. He was hungry. He would have relished a small cigar, but had brought none with him. This craving persuaded him to climb down from the top.

He was halfway to the deck when he saw some men rush forward, near the port bow. Girandole ran over with a spyglass. Two topmen hurried past him up the shrouds. He reached the deck and joined the others at the rail.

In answer to his question, the first mate handed him the glass.

"There is a cask drifting out there, and to the left, a pole that might be an oar."

The chevalier saw the two pieces of wood, floating a cable's length from each other, far off the point of the reefs.

"This does not bode well for Montpassé," he observed, handing back the glass.

Girandole was grave. He made no reply, but immediately went back to scanning the sea for other bits of flotsam. The dinner bell had rung. As he left him, Du Mouchet promised to inform the captain of what had happened.

Neither the first mate nor Colinet after him saw any other signs of wreckage. The cask and the oar—for it was later clearly identified as such—were drifting very slowly northward from a point to the southeast. This course brought them somewhat closer to the ship, though they seemed likely to pass her far out to sea. By the middle of the afternoon, they were still two and a half miles off. It was only around six o'clock that they drifted near the vessel, three cables' lengths off at their closest point. The men watched them until dark, long enough to notice that their course had bent slightly toward the island's northern shore. Then the night swallowed them up.

VI.

BLOCHE HAD DECIDED to give the men a day's grace before cutting their water rations. He no longer awaited the return of Montpassé. What fate had befallen him and his companions? For the moment they had no way of knowing but were not yet willing to admit the worst, and there was speculation that the castaways might still be alive, yet unable to come within sight of the ship.

The captain hoped for some wind and intended to examine the island in the *flûte,* since all their boats were gone. That night there had been a capful of wind, like a puff of hot breath, and to the north, two or three silent flashes had sent amber light billowing into the sky, which had secretly grown overcast. In the morning, there was an incandescent haze in the air, and tattered wisps of pale purple still streaked the eastern horizon. The rivulets of oil snaking across the surface of the water had given way to a lazy suggestion of waves.

Bloche wanted to see these things as signs. Something was brewing not too far away; that day or the next, he thought, might bring a change in the weather.

All the same, this waiting, envenomed by the probable wreck of the jollyboat, darkened everyone's mood. And the numbers of the sick were growing: two the previous evening, and three before noon. The *Entremetteuse* was beginning to stink hellishly. The men took to gazing at the island, never taking their eyes from her, looking her up and down and from end to end. She was only a miserable gunshot away. They imagined leaping that distance to vanish into the foliage.

And so the crew whiled away the day, arguing occasionally about the likelihood of a breeze or what measure to take next. The fishing lines hanging over the rail into the dirty water were checked less and less often, and always came up empty. The gentlemen stayed in their cabins, busy with their little tasks, writing, lazing about; the petty officers hardly budged from the gun room. All were wrapped in solitude and melancholy. Night fell with an awful sense of emptiness and thirst. People began to go around in circles.

At six o'clock, Saint-Foin had gone to see Picot-Fleury. The patient was suffering; he complained of shooting pains and cramps, claiming that he could feel inside himself the bubbling of some vile fermentation. Since that morning he had been vomiting frequently, and his diarrhea had been unrelenting. His voice quavered with agitation and distress.

"Saint-Foin, I am emptying out and there is no end to this. My body could not possibly contain all this filth. Something is spewing it out piecemeal. It is unbearable. Great God, why? Where does all this foulness come from? It must be stopped, Saint-Foin, do you hear me?"

Then, after a prolonged spasm of agony, he had cried out, "Ah! To be rid of these entrails for an hour, even just one hour! To be empty for good and all, as clean and hollow as a mummy!..."

And the surgeon felt the pain in his own belly awaken once again.

As he did each evening, Dominique had come to feed the birds (with a bit of rice snatched from the rats and a few insects that he had patiently hunted down) and to water the last four shoots that still clung to life among fifty withered cuttings. The two escaped parrots had long since disappeared. Dominique assumed they had flown off to the island, and far from regretting their loss, he felt they were now much better off. Moreover, if it hadn't been for his loyalty to his master, he would have willingly freed the others, keeping only one or two in the cause of science.

It was dark beneath the quarterdeck. In the oblique red light of the setting sun, flies zigzagged like sparks shot from a fire. The chattering of the parrots gave a woodsy air to the odds and ends lying about between the guns and the capstan.

There was no one around, aside from three gunners sitting idly on a gun carriage. The sailors had fallen silent at the young man's arrival to watch him, and not a word was said as he fed the birds. Next he had to fill their drinking cups and water the cuttings. He had brought along a bucket and the key to the padlock on the scuttle-butt at the foot of the mainmast. As he prepared to dip out his water, one of the gunners spoke to him.

"Say, chicky, you don't seem to know our water rations is to be cut."

Although Bloche had warned the steward and his mates to keep mum, the news had soon spread through-out the ship.

"Beg pardon?" said Dominique.

"Short rations, lad. And what goes for us, goes for your birds and sticks."

"I have heard nothing of this."

"Me, I'm telling you."

"Fancy that," sniffed Dominique, turning back to his task.

"Let that water be!" shouted the man. "Hey, there! Are you deaf? I told you to let that be!"

Dominique brazenly filled his bucket. The gunner was on his feet in a trice, and taking four quick strides, he grabbed Dominique by the back of the collar and stuck his pitted, hairy face nose to nose with the young man. His breath stank sourly of tobacco and skilly.

"I warrant you'll get my point soon enough, chicky!"

Just then Dominique felt the prick of a knife in his ribs and froze, open-mouthed, his bucket resting on the edge of the scuttlebutt. He smelled the foul breath and gamey odor of the man pressed up against him with clenched teeth and flaring nostrils. Dominique's fear made him strangely torpid; he could hear the water lapping against the ship's side and the violin-hum of the flies drawn to their sweat.

The moment seemed endless...

"That's enough, La Bigorne," said one of the other gunners calmly. "Let him go now."

"Aye, I'll do that," replied his friend. "But first I'd like to see our young gentleman here put back what he's taken."

Then Dominique had an outlandish idea. What if he spilled the water onto the deck? Could he get away without being skewered? His assailant was risking a great deal—perhaps too much for him to leave it at that. If he were afraid of reprisals, whack! He would finish the job. And dump the body discreetly out a porthole. Two men had already vanished that way in heavy weather. You could blame a lot of things on heavy weather! Everyone knew they had been done for in that death trap below decks...But when a ship is lying at anchor, then what? Now this brute would have to think twice about taking a hasty revenge with a cutthroat blow.

The thought of pain suddenly swept aside these speculations. Dominique emptied the bucket into the scuttlebutt and allowed himself to be swung around by La Bigorne, who stuck his fetid mouth right under his victim's nose.

"And now, chicky, take it into your head to put on airs again and I promise you your fill and more of water—

forever. The ocean all to yourself! What do you say to that?"

This incident hastened the execution of a plot that had been brewing for several days. In the middle of the night, someone stole to the foot of the mainmast and blew out the lamp. He was then joined by several shadows in what was now almost total darkness. The only light shone through the slats of a shutter in the passage between the private cabins that lay aft. The shadows groped along, spreading out among the cages and baskets, swearing softly when they bumped into something. There were sounds of wicker creaking, the reedy squawks of parrots, then nervous flutterings of feathers. The shrieks of a few birds were choked off, but others took up the cry, their wings beating like flapping gloves. In spite of all efforts and warnings, the shadows had stirred up a muffled riot. Several times, after a firm "Hush!" they paused to listen. It was not those who slept forward in the waist they feared awakening, but those in the cabins, and especially the one whose candle still burned. This wakeful soul must have been hard of hearing, and the others sleeping soundly indeed, because the shadows were not disturbed. By and by, the screeches of protest died away, and the rest of the operation took place in silence. A shadow appeared before a gunport, slid a basket into the space between the gun and the porthole, and lowered the basket away on a rope passed through the handles. At the neighboring porthole, another shadow did the same.

One by one, the cuttings were unloaded in this way with no more noise than a squeaking of wicker, like the crackle of a small paper fire. Their task accomplished, the shadows slipped down the hatchway behind the mainmast, carrying bundles of feathers.

The next scene was played below. They had decided to roast the birds in the bread oven, which was conveniently located between decks. Besides, while they distrusted the cook, fearing he would spoil their plan, they knew they could easily persuade the baker, Frichoux, with a knife at his back. As he was a good sort, they found him an alibi: he was sent to sleep over by the wheel so that he might be seen by the officer of the watch. At dawn, all traces of the feast were gone, and all flavor of the aviary and the greenhouse had vanished from the jumble around the base of the mainmast.

It was Baudin who discovered the crime. He immediately informed the captain, who sent for Dominique, to inform him in turn. In a fit of indignation, the naturalist's assistant related what had happened on the previous day, stating that one of the men was called La Bigorne, and that he could identify the two others. Bloche was not unhappy at finding an opportunity to cool off a few hotheads. He asked Dominique to retire to his cabin and ordered the muster of all hands at eleven o'clock.

Just a small group of malcontents had been involved that night, but the news had quickly spread. When the bosuns came piping and bawling down the hatchways, only a few of the men were still ignorant of the affair. Their mates let them in on the secret, so that everyone knew what was up when they mustered in the waist.

The fifty able-bodied men waiting for the captain were bathed in a milky light. Most of them wore only woolen caps and trousers fringed at the knees. Gaunt or fleshy, tanned or rosy, well-built or spindle-shanked—there were all sorts, and all with crimson faces that made a strange showing in the sunshine. There was Mâche-fer, with his hammerhead; the hatchet-faced Bat-la-lame, whose chin almost dragged along the ground; Chaudet and his great beak; Espinglet, whose eyes were as round as buttons; the Iroquois with his rough-hewed features; Manoque, as pockmarked as a sponge; Bourdicaud, whose face was all beard; Ramberge, who wore a black patch over his dead eye; Petrel, with his caved-in mug; Muchard, whose nose was nothing more than two holes...

Flanked by his two officers, Bloche strode across the quarterdeck to address the men. Standing by the ship's bell, between the barricade and the mainmast, he struck a stern pose: with his tricorn set squarely on his head and his big belly thrust forward, he glared bullishly at his crew, who fell silent. Still he waited, the corners of his mouth drawn down as though by a bit. There were no sounds but the creaking of the ship, the distant cries of the birds over the reefs, and the rumble of the breakers.

"Was it not enough?" he said finally. "Three of our number are carried off by scurvy, Monsieur de Mont-passé is wrecked, all our boats are lost, we are helplessly becalmed. Is that all? It is not! A greater evil now threatens us."

He paused, and his gaze swept the crowd. No one flinched. Several of the men smiled surreptitiously; the others did their best to look angelic.

"It seems that some of you wish to turn this ship into a bedlam!"

He paused again, and more than one listener began to think he might be overdoing it. He couldn't fool them: he was going to blow the incident out of all proportion as an excuse for cutting their rations.

The captain pointed a threatening finger and raised his voice even higher.

"Do not think, my friends, that I will allow you to grow lax in the performance of your duties for some fool reason or other. This dead calm, the heat, the sickness on board—what of them? Are they not part of a sailor's lot in life? Here infraction of the rules is a crime, for which I have but one remedy: discipline. Yes, gentlemen! It is my duty to impose it on you, as it is yours to submit to it. And I shall increase the dose as the disorder worsens. Have no fear: on this score I am a physician without equal."

Was he ever going to get to the point?

"Last night, the cuttings and parrots of Monsieur Picot-Fleury disappeared. I expect the perpetrators of this crime to come forward."

Silence.

"If they do not, I shall not beat about the bush, I warn

you. The innocent must then suffer with the guilty. But perhaps every one of you is a party to this deed?"

More silence.

"Is this what I am to understand?"

Still, silence. They could see through his ruse: he thought it clever to tighten his hold on them, to call it punishment rather than necessity.

"One last time: is every one of you involved in this conspiracy?"

Now there's a fine question! Give it up, Captain. Just cut the water ration and be done with it.

"Well, gentlemen, since you would have it so, I shall stop your tafia until further order."

The men were dumbfounded. Bloche had blindsided them. Instead of a frontal attack—on their water—he had stabbed them meanly in the back. Surprise and indignation surged through the crowd.

"What?" they shouted. "No tafia?"

"But, Captain, without tafia the vermin will get us, sure!"

"It kills the foulness. We'll all be done for!"

"Don't do it, Captain!"

"Anyway," shouted someone, "them twigs was all dead!"

"Aye! They ought to of gone by the board a long time ago."

"Aye! Aye!" cried several voices. "And them parrots ought to of been ate as well!"

Then another voice rang out.

"And our water, Captain? What about our water?"

Everyone heard him and fell silent. Bloche seemed inclined to reply but took his time, scanning the audience with that fishy eye of his.

"I had not finished. For I must correct this most dangerous drift of yours, which cannot be allowed further indulgence. Therefore, in addition, the scuttlebutts will be stowed away, shielded from your greedy stares, and every man's water ration shall be cut to two pints per day."

Even though they had expected this restriction (now disguised as a punishment), the crew protested anew. They lumped everything together—the reduced water ration, the loss of their tafia—and directed their resentment against cruel fate, the captain, the naturalist's cuttings, and that stagnant water they would have to drink plain.

"Of course," continued Bloche, speaking over the hubbub, "I am ready to review these measures if it turns out that you are not all guilty. I did not think so. Moreover, before you dissuaded me from pursuing this tack, I had sure means of unmasking several amongst you. But you seem so bound to charge yourselves all in a body that I hesitate, I admit, to press on. Perhaps we should go no further in this matter. Monsieur de Girandole, what is your opinion?"

The men did not understand, but suspected a trick. If Bloche could produce the guilty ones, why had he tarred them all with the same brush? He was deceiving them, surely, going at it hit or miss, and knew nothing.

Many were convinced of this. Not La Bigorne, who suspected that the "chicky" had squawked. All Bloche's fancy talk meant nothing to him. He had a feeling that the old man would jump on him in the end, so he decided to take the initiative.

"Captain!" he shouted, to the surprise of his mates. "I don't know who did it, but I can tell you this: I ate some parrot and I'm not sorry for it. After all the slop we've been fed, it went down easy, you can believe me."

"What is your name?"

"La Bigorne."

"Hm!…Duquesne or Dumaine, called La Bigorne, are you not?"

"Dufresnes, Captain."

"So, you happened to receive a portion of fowl without knowing whence it came. Strange, no?"

"It was dark."

"Indeed! However, I had intended to make a meal of this poultry myself, you see. In short, you took this food right out of my mouth."

"'Tis sorry I am to hear that, Captain."

"You have robbed me, Dufresnes."

"That were not my intention."

"'Tis all the same."

"Then punish me!" exclaimed the sailor angrily. "I don't regret it one bit. For days we been eating swill, spoiled vegetables and stinking fish, and now to cap it, we'll not even have tafia to wash down this muck. Captain, I don't want to rot on my feet. But the way we're heading, that's what it's coming to. And when I see crabs making eyes at me, I have to start looking out for myself…"

"I ate some parrot too!" shouted one of his companions. "And I'm like La Bigorne: not sorry I done it. Maybe even it might pull me through."

"Me too!" cried another. "And 'tis more useful in my belly than in them cages."

There was a great clamor, in which one man after another could be heard denouncing himself. The crew was emboldened, and began making recriminations; in another moment, even those who had taken no part in the feast would have been claiming complicity. Then, carried away by the general excitement, a tall, thin fellow with shoe-button eyes went too far.

"Me too, Captain," he called shrilly. "I even went along with La Bigorne, Farignon, and the rest to wring them birds' necks."

At these words, a sudden chill fell over the crowd. Everyone looked to see who had spoken: that idiot Espinglet. They turned toward Bloche, whose mouth was working as though he were trying to free a crumb caught between two teeth. His gray eyes looked off into the distance while he savored the silence.

"Monsieur Dufresnes," he said finally, "the man named Farignon, and you there, who just piped up in so timely a fashion—come here. I shall proceed no further. You three will pay for all the others. Monsieur de Girandole, they are condemned to run the gantlet."

"How many times, Captain?"

"One only. I think they will fully enjoy tasting a rope's end at the hands of those who ought to be punished with them. As for the lot of you," he added, pointing threateningly at the others, "I restore your allowance of tafia, but remember this well, should the mere idea of insubordination even cross your minds: therein lies the greatest evil that can befall you. And now, you will place yourselves at the disposal of Monsieur de Girandole."

The sentence was carried out immediately under the command of the first mate. Short ropes called colts were distributed to thirty men, who formed themselves into two parallel lines in the waist. The condemned men then ran, one at a time, between these lines. The blows to their backs were laid on with a will...

Bloche did not stay to witness this scene. He had gone off to his dinner. The truth was, he wished to avoid the spectacle, for he did not like these overly brutal punishments in which men debased themselves, bawling like calves, or gritting their teeth and swelling with cold rage almost to apoplexy. He had had to order similarly harsh chastisement only twice before during the voyage: once for a serious knife wound inflicted during a brawl, and again for the attempted desertion of four sailors. He preferred confinement, which allowed the condemned man time to mend his ways without too much resentment. On this occasion, he had needed to make an example of the offenders and felt that locking up a few troublemakers would not have been enough to persuade the others to fall back into line.

During dinner, little was said about the incident. The chevalier regretted only that this fresh meat should have escaped his grasp, and Malestro, upon learning of the punishment meted out to La Bigorne, one of his confederates (along with Ramberge), showed an icy indifference. As for Trinquet, who never paid any attention to such domestic problems, he declared unexpectedly that he thought the penalty too light. No one asked Picot-Fleury for his opinion...

The afternoon wore on beneath that glowing white veil drawn across the sky. The sun's light, thus diffused, flowed like water over a globe, dazzling men's eyes with black spots. It was stifling. The air was as thick as plaster, and it was impossible that this breathless heat should not presage some violent change. The ocean seemed soiled with clay. The island was flattened out, like a tortoise shell.

They waited for rain, but none came. It simply refused to fall. It stayed aloft, as still as the creamy dust that haymaking sends floating into the air, gorged with light, flooding the universe all the way up to the sun.

At four o'clock a man died. Two hours earlier, he had begun bleeding from the nose. He had swelled up, hemorrhaging under the skin, and then had been stricken with a bloody flux. His flesh had split open in places; his life was running out of him everywhere. He had not screamed, or moaned, or wept, seized as he was by a terrible astonishment.

His burial service was held soon afterward. The men had reassembled on deck beneath that crushing sun, in the powdery light sifting endlessly down upon them, bleaching everything, and the shroud seemed dusted with sand, as though it had itself just been unearthed. This bath of light had a strange association with death.

The men were grim. It was no longer a question of mourning some poor fellow who had run out of luck. They were all in it now. Each one of them stared at the winding-sheet of sailcloth and thought that another one just like it might soon be cut for him. What should they do? Wait for the wind? And then? What if the island were inapproachable? Ah, what a fine idea it had been to come sit drooling in front of it. True, the isle was beautiful. And wondrous things were there—cool, sweet, pulpy, fragrant things. Just the thought of them made you feel suddenly hot all over. But this beauty was as inaccessible as a woman in a harem, to be possessed only with the eyes...Unless a lovely great sheltered bay lay on the other side, waiting to be taken. Who could say for sure there wasn't? Only Montpassé knew. Perhaps...

The cook's plank tilted; the dead man vanished over the side. Some white birds soaring a cable's length away were drawn by the splash. They sailed over the gently churning water, then tarried, gliding about the ship. The men watched them with sympathy—the sympathy of a wolf for its nice, plump prey—until a bosun declared that they had smelled the corpse. The crew's hatred flared up. They urged Bloche and the officers to fetch the guns. Colinet ran off and brought back two muskets. The birds were still there. The first two shots, one after the other, scattered them to the four corners of the sky, but the captain had hit one of the birds. Fluttering clumsily in its efforts to flee, it fell, at a distance of thirty toises.

The men ran to the rail. The bird had landed lopsidedly, with one wing extended. The water around it was stained with pink. The bird did not move, except when shaken periodically by a brief convulsion. Bloche reloaded his gun. He took aim. This shot was a direct hit: the bird rolled over with the impact and collapsed in its pool of blood. It was no more than a little tangle of shattered flesh floating on the deep blue sea. The men lost interest in it.

Later, the carcass drifted well to the north, where it suddenly disappeared. It had been snapped up without the slightest ripple. There was nothing left but a pinkish swirl of water and two tiny white specks.

VII.

THE NEXT DAY, the veil of clouds was gone. Glazed once more with the purest blue, the sky stretched endlessly over the inky depths below.

It was maddening. There was something sullen, obstinate, hostile in the wind's refusal to blow. Although they had been becalmed before—and had suffocated in those ghastly black broths that confound sea and sky, making it impossible to glimpse the rigging groaning overhead or even to see one's feet—they had never so felt the cruelty of it.

The day before, the haze had seemed to increase the heat. Now, with a clear sky, it was worse. Like an infernal machine, the sun was firing up in the void. It discharged floods of boiling oil. It screamed at white heat, deafeningly, incessantly. Nothing moved on that languid water. Nothing but a vast incandescence filled the air.

Seven men reported to the sick bay. Three of them had running sores or swellings that were treated with white ointment and Goulard's extract. The other four were scorbutics whom Saint-Foin assigned to cots, despite the grumbling of Robinot. They pushed the bulkheads out one last time. They could not be moved any farther. New patients would have to be left to lie in their hammocks.

The great space between decks was full. The crew preferred stewing in their own sweat to shriveling up like fish hung to dry on a rack. They slouched over to the portholes, dreaming of marble and cool springs. That beanpole Bat-la-lame had stripped naked and was sitting gingerly on the very edge of a chest, fanning his hollow chest, his red armpits, and his drooping genitals. A few of the men were flat on their backs on the planking, their arms outstretched, and they lay there staring up at the deck beams—as long as a fly didn't bother them, or a cockroach crawl within striking distance. Tire-sec and Quérole were the only men quietly playing cards. Someone was engraving a bottle with a nail, which screeched plaintively. Bracing himself against the side of the ship, Mâche-fer was trying to dig a molar out of his jaw with a pocketknife, of which only the handle could be seen. Perhaps it was his chagrin at having to spoil his lovely set of horsy teeth, as much as the pain, that put those tears and that ferocious glare in his eyes. Finally, there were La Bigorne, Farignon, and Espinglet, sitting or lying prone, their backs raw from the flogging, philosophically digesting the affront of their punishment at the hands of their mates. For their part, they would have laid on the blows every bit as heartily: justice must not play favorites...

Occasionally, someone walked slowly forward to the

head. For a long time now, the men had stopped going through the sick bay to the open prow. If they needed the seat of ease—for they emptied their bladders over the side—they crossed the forecastle, climbed over the bulwark, and went down along the bowsprit to the grating.

They returned the same way, without meeting a soul. Aside from the officer of the watch, who found a hundred reasons to be elsewhere, the waist, the quarterdeck, and the forecastle were deserted. The crew went there only to dash buckets of water on the deck and the rigging, which made the ship steam like a tureen of piping hot soup.

Malestro had been observed at the starboard bow, however, studying the island at length through a glass.

Then Du Mouchet had come prowling around. He soon joined the ship's writer, who pointed out to him three specific spots on the island's flank. They were three similar trees, their palm leaves fanned out like an Indian headdress, swimming in silvery reflections.

The entire island shimmered in the light, soaking up sunshine even with her violet shadows. The foliage of glossy green leather glittered like teardrop earrings. The island offered herself to her aggressors, swooning in the heat, her fountain gushing an invitation to lips, tongues, throats. The chevalier ran the spyglass slowly over the isle, and lingered at the cascade. But all that water going to waste out of reach exasperated him. He looked away. Almost directly before the ship, a long, green meadow opened a clearing all the way to the edge of a sharp rise topped with a large, shady tree and a great tangle of tall plants, a vantage point that seemed to look out over the lagoon, the tip of the reef, and the dense greenery of the bluffs. There were promises of cool shade, the clean scent of grass, fruits as ripe and heavy as milk-swollen breasts. There were indolent delights, enough for a hundred years...

The chevalier handed the glass back to Malestro and soon wandered off. He climbed to the foretop, where he discovered a topman lying in the shadow of the mast. He tried the maintop, only to find another topman. Wishing neither to oust them nor to remain in their company, he climbed down again and went off to visit Trinquet.

Opening his door, the old man removed his spectacles to rub his swollen eyes. He was wearing an open dressing gown and a long cap of coarse cotton.

"Come in," he said, stepping aside.

At once Du Mouchet smelled a mixed odor of musty linen and old candlewax. The place was quite cluttered: a small bookcase with lattice doors, a table laden with large books and a pile of charts, a writing desk covered with sheets of paper, a chest, an armchair, a pitcher in a basin, a rumpled shirt and stockings lying across a pair of shoes.

Trinquet returned to his chair and waved the chevalier to a seat on the berth.

"One moment, I pray you," he said. "I am just finishing this passage."

He began to write in a rapid scrawl, squinting closely

at the paper, fumbling for the opening in his inkwell whenever he wished to dip his pen.

The chevalier was near the table. He looked over at the charts, carelessly heaped up, with some of the rolled ones crumpled. He imagined Cornelius pushing them about, rummaging among them as though they were useless old paper, without sparing even the portolanos, whose colored edges could be seen peeking from the mess. That was his way, this impatience, this befuddled agitation he brought to everything.

One of these charts was spread out over the others and weighted at either end by a compass and a pewter candlestick. On its soiled and foxed paper, the rays of two suns intersected, and a large ornamental vignette, conveniently placed to mask uncertain shores, could not make up for all the cartographer's ignorance. Here and there, lines thickened by shading ended out in the middle of the ocean. It was as though they had vanished into the paper, drawn but invisible. The strangest effect came from entire regions sketched in this manner and thus appearing as a void. The sea dissolved into land, and the land into water, like basins flooded by a river in spate, where the riverbed is indistinguishable from the inundated fields.

The chevalier considered these scraps of land wrested with such difficulty from the unknown. "These islands whose positions are revealed," he thought, "these shores we rush to record—are we not to them as madams who sell dearly the virginity of their girls? Should we not keep them secret, or situate them elsewhere? Navigators are known—albeit for base reasons—to keep them in their own custody. Still, perhaps 'tis better than to make whores of them. What is the use of soiling the blue of maps?..."

Trinquet stabbed out a final period, set down his pen and his eyeglasses, and turned his chair toward his guest.

"You see well enough to write, then?" asked the chevalier.

"I manage. It is rereading what I have written that gives me trouble."

"Do not be stubborn, Cornelius. Consult Saint-Foin."

"Nay! Saint-Foin is but a poisoner. My remedy suits me. It is only this damned sea that galls my eyes."

The chevalier took out a tinderbox and a case he had thought to bring with him. He lighted his second cigar of the day.

"Are you still inclined to believe that this is Valmate's island?" he inquired.

"I have been given to think that this topic is out of season."

"Come, now, what do you say?"

"If you must know, you need only read my paper to the Ministry of Longitude."

"Very well. I see at least that you have taken enough interest in the island to mention it in your writings."

Trinquet looked over at the porthole, and the chevalier kept silent, knowing that the old man would soon warm to his subject.

"You see," continued Trinquet with more energy, "these islands are not our concern. Although one might— for want of anything better, you will say—give them a passing glance. For every island like this one there are a score just like it: a navigator spots one, takes the bearings of the place, publishes them, and presto! No one ever hears any more about it. What must we think? That these islands do not exist? That the navigator was seeing things? That those who came afterward looked in the wrong place? Or is this silence the work of those miserable scoundrels who conceal their discoveries or knowingly place them elsewhere?"

"Of course," agreed the chevalier. "But ascertaining the position of a place in this boundless ocean is hardly easy. Everyone makes mistakes. Have we not ourselves been occasionally in error?"

"Stop right there, Jacques! I myself was responsible for the charts and the ship's chronometer. A hydrographer with such instruments at his disposal furnishes documentation wholly different from that of some wretch who simply follows his nose."

"That was yesterday. Today, the chronometer is out of order, and you no longer care at all about our route."

"True."

"This island we have chanced upon—who knows when others will find it again?"

Trinquet raised a cautious hand to show how vague this prospect was.

"Oh, my friend, that is another matter. True, I must now work with no more than what I am given. To identify this island, I had to place my confidence in sailors who have been muddling these matters for centuries. You understand my prudence. The longitude, under these circumstances, is quite fanciful, and I do fear that any official undertaking to establish more accurate calculations will have its work cut out for some time."

"And Valmate's figures?"

"Why do you think this island has been impossible to find for so long? They are false, of course! Such things have thrown us into this perpetual imbroglio. Losing themselves from island to island, these foolish sailors have mistaken one for another, making endless corrections and giving names to places already baptized. So here we are now, wondering at each isle if she is this one's Jeanne, that one's Marion, or someone else's discard. It's no wonder we are all at sea. Sometimes a real island ceases to exist, sometimes another springs full blown from a geographer's imagination."

"A pure invention? Now there you go too far. How could that be?"

"Quite easily. Let us take the case of Antilia. This island was born of the fevered imagination of a Florentine enamored of astronomy. It was nothing more: a simple name tossed out by chance and awaiting a taker. Along comes Cristobal to the Americas and snatches it up. Done! The chimera becomes real, and the astronomer enters the Pantheon. So you see, my friend, in the union of their dreams, Columbus and Toscanelli gave birth to an island…"

The chevalier smoked his cigar, gazing thoughtfully at his old tutor, whose hollow cheeks were deeply etched by wrinkles. Behind his stiff appearance, there was a kind of cool, tenacious enthusiasm, something that always took pleasure, despite the wear and tear of age, in tinkering with ideas.

They talked some more, with Cornelius ranging widely over different lands, sailors, scholars, and the odd paradox, but never touching on the present dangerous situation. The chevalier was disappointed. Several times he wanted to interrupt and say, "Stop this, Cornelius. You may well meet your end here, before this island, and no one will know anything of your speculations." After all, what could these scribbled pages reveal? What did they report besides his wanderings?

For he had wandered far and wide all during that campaign. Oh, it was a noble quest: to find a continent, that famous austral continent held by learned men in the Old World to be the counterpart to the boreal lands. Cornelius had believed in its existence so fervently that he had sent—at great expense—for one of those marine chronometers, the design of which was then being perfected, and with the blessing of the Ministry of Longitude, he had convinced the chevalier to fit out the expedition.

"He still believes in this fantastic continent," reflected Du Mouchet. "And if we had not torn him from his stubborn searching, he would have utterly exhausted both his strength and ours. He resents this and is angry with us. He persists in ignoring our pressing need to return. This man is blinded by his dreams. We have saved him in spite of himself. Perhaps…"

The Traveler's Tree

After a last puff on his cigar, he stubbed it out in the saucer of the candlestick and took leave of the old man.

He went up to his cabin, reflecting that he truly had no use for geography. A fig for the Ministry of Longitude and all those cosmographers with their endless ratiocination! "Our mission," Cornelius had called it.

"Not so fast!" thought the chevalier. Yes, the old man's plan had seduced him. Yes, he had opened his coffers for him, and had removed a storeship from the Pinson fleet. But when the hydrographer had spoken to him, one day during the campaign, about his fear that the chevalier would betray "their mission" for one or another of these islands, he had sent his former tutor back to his dear books. True, after much wandering, fickleness, and disillusionment, he had come quite close to reconsidering the purpose of the expedition. A fine thing! They had been chasing the wind all along, just as they still were, with nothing but a collection of names to show for it.

Back in his cabin, he took off his shirt and lay down on his bed, where he reflected that people set great store by all these names. He himself had never given one to any of the islands he had conquered. In his brief journal entries, he referred to each island simply as *she,* but the clarity of his memories was undimmed. He remembered the scents of every one, and the coves, the rounded hillocks, the pelage of vegetation. Much to his surprise, he felt waves of nostalgia, but understood that these feelings sprang not from the islands—had he not said time and again that he had seen everything there was to see of them, one and all—but from the pleasure he had taken there, a faceless pleasure, separated from its object. And while he had not forgotten what belonged to each island, he wished to remember only moments of sensual delight.

He fell into a reverie. There came to him scatterings of raindrops, bramble scratches, the coolness of small gorges, strange odors steeping in slimy marshes, abrupt pathways through lush forests, flowers, mosses, fruits that opened like mouths, warm breezes, burning depths, the sighing of branches, hurried steps through long ravines, the clattering of palms, furious rustlings, the heady flash of brilliant birds, the sticky heat and pounding heart after a chase, falling asleep in the tall gray grasses...

Around four o'clock he heard a sudden, soft thump on the planking in front of his door. He went out on deck. A man had just collapsed. He lay with his face twisted back over his shoulder and one hand in the air. The chevalier took him for dead, as did all the others who ran up. They thought he had suffered the same fate as the master carpenter. It was chilling, the way this sickness could cut a man down without warning.

In fact, the man had only fainted. He had dawdled at the rail, gazing at the island, and the sun had set his brains to cooking in his skull. Robinot revived him with two buckets of seawater and a swallow of rum, then had him carried below. There was a death, however, late that afternoon: a servant, a solitary, painstaking, and tidy man who always wore a wig with the tail curved up like a curtain hook. Several days earlier, a great lump had puffed up behind his knee, his feet had swollen, and his ankles, knees, and elbows had begun to ache. One morning he was found on a ladder, in a daze. He did not even seem to be suffering, but when they tried to take hold of him, he began to pant, as though he had a hot potato in his mouth.

They were sitting up late in the great cabin, with all the windows open. Mosquitoes and tiny moths flitted about the candles, their wings crepitating in the flames. In the distance could be heard the cooing of innumerable birds. To wash away the nasty taste of the supper—only two miserable little blue fish had been caught that day, at dawn, and gobbled up at dinner—they were savoring the very noble and very old sweet wine of Caine, with its floral bouquet, its aroma of caramel and faint earthy fragrance. Bloche was sprawled in his chair, tired and thoughtful. On the gallery, the chevalier was smoking one of the three cigars he had thriftily decided to allow himself each day from then on. Trinquet was bathing his eyes while Saint-Foin looked on in distress, and Malestro was playing chess with Girandole, in a game he had already won. They had almost forgotten the anxiety that gnawed more and more often at their vitals when Dominique entered and spoke to Saint-Foin.

"Monsieur, my master is very ill. You must come."

The surgeon left immediately; a few quick steps brought him to the naturalist's cabin. He was followed by the chevalier, and then Girandole.

Picot-Fleury lay trembling with fever on his cot, his

sheets soaked with sweat. There was a vile smell of putrid diarrhea. His livid face was wasted and drawn, as though the skin were pulled taut by claws. His eyes were closed. He was moaning.

"Speak to me," said Saint-Foin.

Picot-Fleury opened his eyes, but did not say a word. When Saint-Foin raised the patient's shirt, the stench became appalling. The abdomen was a bluish color, hard and swollen.

"Dominique, go to the sick bay. Ask Robinot for some saltpeter and some simarouba bark. Fetch as well some toilet water and an enema nozzle. That will do. Girandole, please ask a servant to heat a bucket of seawater."

Dominique had left. Girandole was not unhappy to do likewise.

"Monsieur Du Mouchet," added Saint-Foin, "nothing obliges you to remain here."

"Do you need assistance?"

"Most certainly, but Dominique will return shortly and—"

"What must be done?"

"Well, then, first we should remove these soiled linens so that he does not lie in his own excrement."

They busied themselves with this amid a swirl of nauseous odors. Saint-Foin paused for a moment when he saw large blotches of half-dried blood in the liquid waste beneath the patient. Returning to his task, he moved more slowly, musing out loud.

"Poisoning or dysentery. One or the other!...The

ipecac, the bleedings, the vesicatories—all that is correct. Why did the colic worsen? With this hemorrhage, an enema is impossible. We would clean him out like a rabbit. First the simarouba. To bring the fever down. But good God, which fever is it?"

They had managed to sit the patient up and remove his shirt and bedclothes. He was still shivering, and his head bobbed mechanically. His face was abruptly distorted by a painful grimace, which yet seemed at the same time a smile of ease. His entire body contracted. Something gurgled beneath him, then burst out all over the mattress. With a terrible, hoarse groan, he collapsed on his side.

Dominique returned with the drugs. Saint-Foin immediately administered the simarouba, handing back the saltpeter and nozzle.

"Return these, they are useless. And ask Robinot for some laudanum and a lancet. Take these linens away. Find me some fresh ones and a good, thick draw-sheet."

After Dominique had left again, Saint-Foin poured a little toilet water into the hollow of his hand and began to rub the sick man's abdomen.

His movements gradually grew slower, and he gazed into that fleshless face, so thin that it seemed to have been eaten away from the inside.

"What have you come up with for me, my dear Picot? Scurvy is the order of the day, did you not know that? Not this mixture of fever and looseness. Must you try so very hard to be different? Oh, I know you and your fondness for unique cases, unclassifiable species…You will not beat me. I will classify you, my friend, I promise you I will!"

He continued to rub him until the bucket of hot water was brought. Dominique returned soon afterward, and while the chevalier watched from the cabin doorway where he had retreated, the other two men washed and dressed their patient only to have their efforts undone by a new rush of blood.

Saint-Foin bled the sick man from his foot, gave him laudanum to drink, had the draw-sheet and thick bundles of linen placed under his buttocks, and covered him with a coarse cloth. Then he committed him to Dominique's care and left, accompanied by the chevalier.

"I am deeply concerned," said Saint-Foin after a few moments. "What stinks there is not this morbid diarrhea. That I can accept. Let me explain: I mean only that it does not alarm me. No, you see, what stinks there, what I dread most terribly, is that almost sweet smell. It is a thing of corpses. I know it—oh, yes! I know it well. And I know, alas, what it means…"

A short while later, Picot-Fleury stopped shivering. The drugs had plunged him into a torpor from which he emerged only long enough to indicate feebly, with a slight movement of his mouth, that he was thirsty.

During the night, the fever returned, and he was mercilessly wrung by dysentery. At daybreak, his breathing was scarcely perceptible. Large discolorations had broken out all over his body. He died before dawn.

VIII.

ENCLOSED IN A HASTILY constructed wooden box, Picot-Fleury's body sank into a filthy brew. Day after day, the *Entremetteuse* had been fouling the water around her, turning it into a stagnant sewer in which stewed gobs of yellowish foam, wood shavings, twists of oakum and hemp, curdled puddles of food scraps, ashes, tobacco-stained spittle, lint bandages blotched with brown, pink dressings, firewood and straw clotted with slime, clabbered vomit, spreading pools of feces, indefinable purple or green or whitish deliquescences, and, floating on the surface, the oily iridescence of scorbutic urine. Heated by the sun, this wallow gave off a frightful stink. It was not enough to have rotting barnacles clinging to the sheathing, or the swampy, carrion reek rising from the hold and the well; there were also these drifting odors to contend with, odors thick enough to touch. The men began looking to see if something had died nearby. They nosed around the sick bay, smelled their soup, sniffed themselves—afraid to find they were rotting without knowing it. Sometimes they lost track of it, but at the slightest turn of the head or deep breath, the same shuddering stench filled their nostrils.

The cloudy drinking water had also seriously deteriorated. The tafia no longer masked its dreadful bitterness, and white worms were turning up more and more frequently in the mugs—some of them half a finger long. The men rebelled against this poison, and against their own need. Was this the precious wealth so carefully rationed by their superiors? Were they degrading the crew to the point of stinting them even in this slop? And their damned thirst drove them to crave such horror! Ah, cool water lapped from a rippling falls...Ah, golden juices, perfumed nectars, the pale milk of a coconut with its two pierced eyes, and flowing from its mouth, its exquisite freshness, its smooth, rich savor, its hint of flowery sweetness...Thirst buffeted them like a calf butting the udder. A fig for dreams! Their longing for this poisonous water returned. They forgot their disgust. They doubted it could prove stronger than sheer relief.

Holding their noses, they would drink the water and immediately feel a violent revulsion. This putrefaction that befouled everything it touched was now fermenting inside them. And in spite of this sacrifice, their thirst was unassuaged.

The men began to feel forsaken by heaven and earth. To their hardships and the silence of the wind was added bodily decay. All, enfeebled and morose, showed signs of scurvy. They limped, whimpered, slavered all day long, and their gravely ill companions, no longer isolated for lack of space, offered an ever-present spectacle of the tortures that lay ahead. What was left to put a bit of heart into them? Certainly not that vile skilly, now no more than a few mashed beans, a portion of rancid salt pork or cod, and one ship's biscuit for every two men. And it was this last insult that raised indignant protests. Although they knew full well the food had rotted in the hold, they could hardly believe so little of it remained. The most levelheaded among them complained of the steward's excessive prudence, while the rest of the crew spoke knowingly of hidden reserves. They distrusted the steward's mates, the officers, the cook, and aired their grievances endlessly at every meal.

That day at dinner tempers flared among a handful of men gathered around a mess bowl. After eating a few spoonfuls, Ramberge suddenly exploded in anger and disgust. He spat out his mouthful and began shouting. Then he grabbed a handful of the mush and stalked off toward the galley. No one followed his example, but a few followed him, happy to find a champion for their discontent.

Ramberge heaped abuse on the cook and tried to shove the fistful of skilly in his face. The cook was not a man to give ground. After dodging the stew, he snatched up a cutlass and threatened his one-eyed assailant.

"One move and I'll stick you!" he snapped.

Refusing to back off, Ramberge whipped out his knife

and brandished it, only to have his thumb sliced open from wrist to nail by the cook's cutlass. The gunner dropped his knife. Blood spurted from the wound, dripping down onto the planking. He cradled his reddened hand and glared at the weapon fallen at his feet.

"Try again and I'll run you through!" warned the cook, holding the sword in front of him with both hands, as though it were a saber.

Ramberge was not so foolishly blinded by rage as to get himself skewered. He took two steps back and spat off to the side. Then he turned and strode away.

The matter might have rested there if Lagarde, a bosun's mate, had not heard the gunner yelling and seen him return with his bloodied hand, followed by a few indignant companions. When the mate questioned the injured man, he was roundly insulted.

This was too much. Ramberge paid for this lapse with ten lashes and was packed off to the lions' den.

Bloche was keeping a tight hand over the men, and they took this as but one more stifling torment. At any other time, they would have seen justice in the punishment, but now they thought it mere cruelty. Had this swine nothing better to do, they muttered among themselves, than to shove their heads underwater? Could he not work on saving their skins?

Bloche was working on it. And while the crew was learning of the deaths first of Ropars (a caulker and a fine, jolly fellow who never missed an opportunity to reminisce, good-naturedly, about the truly charming island girl from whom he had caught an embarrassing disease), and then Franchomme (a carpenter as strong as a horse, built to last a hundred years, yet carried off by scurvy in eight days), and while Ramberge was listening to the burning complaint of his shoulders, the captain was informing his officers of his decision to build a raft.

They had all thought of this. It was the only way left for them to explore the island and attempt a landing. Although Bloche had burned his fingers badly over the failure of the two previous expeditions, his mind was made up, and he raged at having no spare boat at his disposal.

Ah, the pinnace would certainly have made things easier, and the memory of its loss awakened hatred and bitterness in the men. Hadn't that been the beginning of their misfortune? Hadn't fate turned against them that day?

The tragedy had occurred a month before, on a large inhabited island. They had been warmly welcomed. Dugout canoes had paddled out to the ship to trade. Bananas and black piglets were exchanged for brimming glasses of wine or broad axes. A little later, crewmen bought the women's favors with nails.

When sailors had tried to recover some stolen articles, however, the natives' threatening gestures had convinced the captain not to linger. He intended to victual and water the ship and depart. The following day, while Girandole and Malestro went off in the longboat to trade ashore, the pinnace left with a load of empty casks for a watering place spotted the day before. Comblezac had been in command of the watering party, accompanied by the chevalier, Vuché, and ten men armed with muskets.

Their destination was more than a mile off, where a stream ran into a deeply recessed beach in a little cove hidden by projecting rocks. The enclosing reef offered only a narrow passage. Finding the approach inside the cove too shallow to bring the pinnace ashore, they anchored it twenty toises out and formed a chain to unload the casks. A good two hundred islanders had gathered on the beach. Comblezac deployed a double row of armed men while the rest began to fill the casks.

Meanwhile, Du Mouchet and Vuché had taken the liberty of leaving the detachment to proceed along the shore. Vuché had seated himself on a rock a short distance away to sketch the scene, while the chevalier had continued on through a grove of sea grape trees.

A few lesser chiefs pretended to control the unruly throng, at the same time allowing the approach of scantily clad women and girls who gestured provocatively at the men. Some of these natives were quite beautiful, with green eyes and thick shocks of black hair. They all had firm breasts, coppery skin, teeth of ivory, and a feline grace. There was as much charm as savagery in their advances, and the promise of sensual delight in the way they caressed their breasts and crotches, flicked their tongues, and stroked the sailors. It required impossible self-denial to resist their pungent perfume.

The first man to succumb was a topman named

Maurague. He had let a woman get her arms around him, and when she began rubbing her belly against his, he lost his head with excitement. He ripped off the little girdle she was wearing, dropped his gun, and threw himself upon her in the sand. Comblezac shouted and rushed over. It was too late: a native had seized the musket. It took two men to separate Maurague and the woman while the natives looked on, laughing.

Comblezac demanded the return of the weapon. The thief had no such intention and disappeared into the crowd. Unwilling to use force, Comblezac ordered a warning shot fired into the air, which did not frighten the savages, but stirred them to anger. They began to yell. Comblezac told his men to retreat while keeping their weapons trained upon the throng, which allowed them to fall back toward the pinnace. Some of the natives followed them into the water, however, while the others gathered rocks. A few sailors stumbled, wetting their guns. They splashed and floundered in the yellow foam, hunching their backs against the flying stones. All of them reached the pinnace, but some natives, arriving hard on their heels, prevented them from hauling in the grapnel by hanging on to the cablet. Seeing the growing uproar and the rocks beginning to fall thick and fast about him, Comblezac gave the order to shoot a savage.

This sparked the attack. A hail of stones flew from the shore, while the natives close to the pinnace attempted to overturn it. Some sailors shot haphazardly into the mob; others beat with oars upon the heads popping up all

around like devils. Two men who fell into the water at the
same time were immediately seized and drowned by a
group of attackers. Then Comblezac was dragged away
to suffer the same fate. The sailors had no time to reload
their muskets. The islanders stormed the boat and emptied it of men. The water boiled red for a moment, as
though churned by a school of fish.

Vuché did not escape. His boulder was only a hundred
paces from the watering place. When he heard Comblezac
shout, he gathered his things, called to the chevalier, and
started back. At the first gunshot, he stopped. The ensu-
ing uproar made him hesitate. Should he flee or return to
the pinnace and the protection of her crew's guns? By the
time he decided to run to his companions, things were
already going badly for them, and the natives were hurling
stones furiously. At the second shot, Vuché froze. He was
out in the open. Spotting him, a handful of natives gave
chase. With his buckled shoes and his legs as bowed as
climbing vines, Vuché was a miserable runner. He was
caught in the grove of sea grapes and promptly strangled.

As for the chevalier, alerted by the gunfire, he was able
to observe the disastrous affray from a distance and see
how useless and insane his intervention would be. He
watched helplessly as the natives began their attack, and
then he saw a blue figure run through the grove three
hundred paces away, closely pursued by some islanders.
Recognizing Vuché, he instinctively drew his sword. He
was determined to go to the man's aid, but to do so he
had to cross some dense undergrowth and skirt a large

hillock. For a moment, the chevalier stood looking for a way through the brush, thinking meanwhile that he would never arrive in time. He had lost sight of his companion. He listened, at first hearing only the cries of the savages and gunshots from the battle; then the sound of rustling foliage made him turn his head. A man was walking swiftly toward him through the undergrowth. It was Malestro, bareheaded and in his shirtsleeves.

He stopped and called to the chevalier, "Come on!"

"We must save Vuché!"

"Too late, he's dead."

"How do you know?"

"I saw it. Come on, follow me!"

"My God," exclaimed Du Mouchet, sheathing his sword and falling in behind Malestro.

They fled from the watering place. The only sound at their backs was now the shouting of the natives.

"How came you to be here?" asked the chevalier excitedly. "Have they attacked the longboat as well?"

"No."

"Why did you leave them?"

"They had no need of me. I left, intending to join you and return with your party. I heard the noise. I watched the battle from a piece of high ground. Then I caught sight of you. It was as I came to join you that I saw our unfortunate Vuché running, only to fall into their hands."

"Poor Vuché."

"There was nothing I could do. They were out of range of my pistol."

"This is appalling, Malestro. These savages have become enraged. I do not know what happened. All at once, shouting, gunfire...How many men will escape? Perhaps none."

"It is indeed possible that you are the only one."

"Where are you going? To the longboat?"

"No. Girandole must have returned to the ship. But I passed a small village. There are some boats there."

They walked on in silence.

After trudging along for some time, they reached the top of a sparsely wooded rise, at the end of which they spied the ship lying at anchor far out in the bay. They went down to a narrow cove occupied by a few huts. Four dugouts lay beached on the shore. The islanders lazing in the shadows seemed to know nothing of the incident at the watering hole.

Malestro approached an old man sitting on a coconut palm stump and managed to make him understand that they wished to use one of the canoes.

"Give him your hat," he told Du Mouchet.

The native received the present without taking his eyes off the two strangers. He called to his people; men and women ran up and began to jabber.

"What do they want?" asked the chevalier.

"I cannot tell. Follow me," said Malestro, who was backing slowly toward the nearest canoe.

Reaching the craft, he held one of the paddles out to the natives to show that he desired assistance. No one stepped forward. No one opposed their departure, either, and seeing this, Malestro shoved the canoe out in the water and stepped into it, followed by the chevalier. They began to paddle away without any hindrance; the clamor that arose behind them might just as well have been a barrage of insults as a show of protest.

They had covered about a hundred toises when there was a great uproar. Looking back, they saw an angry mob from the watering place running onto the beach, brandishing clubs and gathering stones. The natives had noticed the chevalier's disappearance and had gone looking for him. Piling into the remaining canoes, they set out in pursuit.

A few of them stood in the prows, waving their weapons and shrieking like infuriated apes. Malestro and the chevalier paddled desperately.

"I'll kill at least one of them," muttered Malestro, trusting in his pistol.

A plume of smoke streamed from a gunport on the ship, and a cannon roared. The ball whistled over the fleeing men's heads to land five toises from one of the pursuing canoes. A second shot came close enough to capsize another dugout. This put the natives to flight, and the two men, much relieved, paddled on toward the longboat now flying to their rescue.

Those aboard the ship knew nothing of the incident at the watering hole. Stunned by the news, Bloche resolved to mount an expedition and sought to anchor in front of the watering place. They could not bring the ship in close enough to put the beach within gun range, however, and the chevalier pointed out to the captain that sending in the longboat, however heavily armed, risked causing a second tragedy, since the bay was not deep enough to allow the boat to come in close to the beach. Stones and spears thrown from the shelter of trees would overwhelm the crew before a single one of them had set foot ashore with his musket. Bloche, still furious, sailed back and forth all day before the bay. They could see the undamaged pinnace surrounded by a crowd of natives. There was no trace of the victims, except for Comblezac's tricorn perched atop a devil prancing brazenly across a thwart in the boat.

It was only after the *flûte* had got an offing that the ship's company paid their last respects to Vuché de Beaune, Lieutenant Comblezac, and the two mates and eight seamen who had perished in the massacre in the cove.

Toward half past six o'clock the men's hopes were revived. The sun had sunk behind the bluffs, darkening the island. Pale scraps of mist slipped down from the foliage to obscure the shore, leaving only flat washes of indigo wreathed in swirls of gray. Suddenly, a sailor called loudly for the officer of the watch, urging him to turn his spyglass on a hill where the man claimed to have seen a moving white form. Taking up his glass, Colinet searched among the bushes and low palm trees.

"Look higher, sir," insisted the man. "It went that way, going up along the small hill, on the left. Ought to come out again between the thickets and the ridge."

Colinet swept his glass over a clearing at the edge of a ravine filled with towering cannas. The mist was everywhere. Behind the gray veil he could barely make out the red dot of a large flower, and up at the crest of a tall tree, the straw-yellow specks of its fruit. Finding nothing, he began to wonder if the sailor had been mistaken.

"You were seeing things, my friend," he said at last.

But the other man, one Mavel, stubbornly defended his story. Some sailors had drawn near, and they were more than willing to believe him. They pressed him for details; he had none to give. He simply repeated that he had glimpsed some damned white thing on the hillside and that it had vanished into the thickets and stayed there.

"Might it be a goat, then?" suggested someone.

Well, he wouldn't say no. It had been of a size, and goatlike in its climbing.

This hypothesis was adopted and the deduction followed immediately: the goat had not dropped from the sky. It had been put there. And to put a goat or anything else on this island one had first to go ashore.

Nightfall prevented Colinet from observing the hillside any further. He hurried off to tell the captain the news, which was already spreading throughout the ship. Soon, with an eager enthusiasm that swept all doubts aside, everyone was talking about Mavel's goat.

As for Bloche, he preferred prudence. Later, at the supper table, he let the others tackle the problem.

If they were to believe what the sailor claimed, they

said, and if the man's eyes had not deceived him, then some seafarers had released goats on the island with the intention, as was the custom, of providing resources for sailors in distress. But who were they? Joachim de Valmate, according to his journal, which Trinquet had reread, had not landed on his island. Others, then, must have done so—in secret. Strange philanthropy indeed, to furnish an island with provisions and then keep its existence a mystery.

This mystery did not bother Malestro. He thought— but only to himself—that the visitors had left the livestock for their own use alone and planned to return there on the quiet. This explanation suited him perfectly. Although he showed only a slight edginess, he was beginning to believe in his good fortune: the island was attributed to an explorer named Joachim; people had visited it on the sly; three Ravenalas (the trees he had pointed out to the chevalier) were visible on the only part of the island they could see.

Then Girandole had unknowingly bolstered his interpretation. If these navigators had been lost at sea after putting in at the island, suggested the first mate, that would explain why the world had never learned of their discovery. This shipwreck appealed to the writer: after hiding their loot, and before being swallowed up by the sea, his visitors would have launched the bottle and its message that some time later came into the bay at Caine, and thus into his own hands.

Their speculations went no further, but for Malestro

this was enough. And he resolved to be among those embarking on the raft that Bloche wished to begin building without delay.

The next morning, Bloche summoned the ship's two remaining carpenters. First he inquired about their timber reserves, and the two men spoke of spare masts and yards, timber in the log, blocks, lignum vitae, mahogany, mangrove, spars taken on in the shipyard, and rough timber cut from island to island by Le Cam. They had ample reserves, even though they had recently begun dipping into them because of a lack of firewood. That was all the captain wanted to know. He described a simply designed raft to the men and ordered them to begin work at once, urging them to seek whatever assistance they required from the petty officers.

The carpenters were masters of their craft, and proud of it. They asked Bloche for the help only of the wet cooper and a sailor they knew to be quite clever with ropes.

All morning long, their saws screaked and hummed. The ship had awakened. She was shaking off the torpor of illness, beginning to bustle again, reviving people tormented as much by hopelessness as by the pitiless sun.

At noon, pieces of ripped timber, planks, posts, and large barrels were brought up to the waist. The workers allowed themselves a short rest and ate their dinner basking in the many attentions lavished on them by their companions. They had been served wine from the gentlemen's stores as well as rum, which they wisely set aside for later. Then they lighted their pipes and began to assemble the raft.

They laid their wood atop three strong crosspieces and tied everything together with the longest sections in the middle, so as to form a rounded prow. Next, beneath this platform, they secured two rows of four empty barrels with their bungs plugged. Then they nailed on a deck, along the edges of which they fastened stanchions, whose heads would serve to support the manropes and oars. Bloche had decided— perhaps to show contempt for the unwilling wind—that it was useless to erect a mast. They made do with a steering oar, the crafting and adjustment of which, like the anchoring of the stanchions, took them quite some time.

The raft was finished at sundown. It looked rather impressive, sitting in the middle of the waist, and the two carpenters—forgetting their disappointment at not being able to devote themselves, with less haste, to the more noble construction of a boat—felt that their unfortunate shipmates Le Cam and Franchomme would not have been displeased with it. The staff came to inspect the raft, and Bloche declared himself satisfied.

After nightfall, it was no more than a peculiar construction caressed by the gleam of lanterns and the chalky moonlight. It had occupied everyone's thoughts all day long, save for the single distraction of a death in the sick bay and the speedy burial that followed. Even the phantom goat had preoccupied only Mavel and a handful of men, who looked for it in vain until the last violet streaks of dusk were gone.

The Traveler's Tree

*

They launched the raft at dawn, and all the while the hoists were lowering away, Baudin bellowed at his crew to be more careful. They loaded casks of wine, water, and salt meat, then an anchor, a grapnel, some ropes, and some empty barrels. Six men went aboard, as well as Coridan, a bosun's mate who was showing signs of scurvy but possessed the rare advantage of knowing how to swim. Then it was Girandole's turn; he carried a tinder-box, some touchwood, candles, a spyglass, fishing lines, and two sturdy horse pistols. He also brought aboard some muskets and a small barrel of powder. They wished they could have had the swivel gun, which had gone down with the longboat, for with it they could have informed the ship of the raft's position and its discoveries. As for flags, they took none, having no mast. Finally, Malestro climbed down, with only a pistol slipped inside his belt. Although suspicious of his motives, Bloche had allowed the ship's writer to join the expedition. He knew him to be shrewd and thought to turn this to advantage now. He had simply taken care that his hanger-on, La Bigorne, should not be part of the detachment; the other confeder-ate, Ramberge, was still confined down in the hold.

It had been agreed that Girandole would work his way northwards along the shore, exploring as far as possible, even if it meant going around the entire island. In that case, considering the difficulties of his mission, they esti-mated that it would be two full days before he doubled the southern point.

IX.

AT HALF PAST seven o'clock, the rowers standing on the platform plunged their oars into the water, and the raft bore off over a softly rippling sea the color of tin plate. The hopes of all went with them. The solemn silence at their departure strengthened their impression of escaping from a loathsome vat of fermenting death. They were leaving behind the sinister stench of a lazaretto. They felt a heady surge of freedom, and at once breathed deeply of the good salt air with its whiffs of sandy shore.

For an hour, they skirted a row of coral teeth half a cable's length away, where the waves were dashing with unusual violence. It was as though the emerald lagoon fed on this chewed-up water, stripped of the harshness of the open sea. There was nothing beyond the reef but smooth, naked water upon green sand. The shore was fair, broken here and there by clumps of trees or the trunks of coconut palms, the carapace of a sandbar, or the shells of small brown rocks. Beyond stretched pale lawns and overgrown tangles of grass, and then thickets of logwood and acacias rising toward the hills.

The *flûte* lay a mile off, a bony, yellowish, powdery thing, like a carcass dug up on a beach. The sun was climbing in the sky and beginning to burn the rowers, who were stripped to the waist. Girandole and Malestro had taken off their tricorns, coats, and waistcoats; their shirts were now becoming uncomfortable as well. The sea had gone ink blue once again. They rowed in silence, the raft lumbering along, not built for speed and going down by the bows with each stroke, but this slow pace suited their examination of the island's defenses. They were, so far, impenetrable.

A vast coconut grove edged the shore, the palms so evenly spaced they might have been planted. Above them rose sun-baked meadows, dotted with thorn bushes and spotted here and there by the dusty green of sage and frangipani. Then tall, handsome trees had reappeared with their dense, dark foliage, from which emerged the promontory of bare rock that could be seen from the ship, jutting out halfway up the slope.

It was a great, rough, purplish-brown lump, set among the trees like a rock in a bed of parsley. As the raft followed the curving shoreline, the shape of the headland changed. The lower section became prominent, while the cavity above was crowned with a ledge.

At first, Malestro had paid no attention to it. He was studying a tree to the right of the huge rock, rising from a small shelf hidden from view, a tree seen as yet only from the side but whose habit he thought he already recognized. When the raft had advanced enough for him to see the tree head-on, his suspicion was confirmed: it was a Ravenala, a very large Ravenala whose fan, as stiffly erect as a war bonnet, glittered with steely reflections. His mind raced; he looked quickly back at the promontory. The face appeared. He was staring at the profile of a monkey: the snout, the hollow of the eye, the flat skull, even the massive brow.

He felt a strong surge of heat through his chest as he recited to himself, "Ravenala on the monkey's shoulder." He had found it! This time, he had found it. He laughed, with a nervous, gasping sound that astonished his companions. His thoughts were far away. And so, all this time, the object of his quest had been right before his eyes! It was ludicrous! He had been wandering for so long, and had made so many mistakes…Hadn't he at first taken the Ravenala for a pagan deity, and the monkey for a totem? What madness! It had taken a chance remark by Picot-Fleury to enlighten him: the Ravenala was a tree, commonly called the traveler's tree. That worthy Picot had taken him to see a specimen, had made him drink the insipid, lukewarm water found in the cuplike base of the leaf stalks, gushing out at the prick of a saber. Malestro had been particularly interested to discover that these stalks spread out like a fan—like an open hand. Another revelation! But one that brought with it gnawing uncertainty. What if he had missed the right tree? And then, that damned monkey, whatever could it be? The totem could be easily discarded in favor of some geographical formation, but a monkey's shoulder—what would that look like? Many a time, studying one of these Ravenalas, he had thought he'd seen something very like it, and half of them had so convinced him that he had set to digging. How much simpler it had turned out to be! An island, a tree, and a crag. Yes, quite simple, if one knew how and where to look...

He returned to his examination of the huge fan and its surroundings. "Thirty paces straight from his open hand." To be counted in one direction or the other, and with other trees he had paced off in both. Here, however, on the one side it was barely eight to ten paces to an escarpment that plunged into dense brush. And on the other? Foliage obscured the area; he could see nothing.

Ignoring his companions, who were intrigued by his concentration, he seized the spyglass. Despite the closer view afforded by the lens, he could make out only a rampart of small leathery leaves, behind which spread the branching limbs of a tall and massive tree. What lay between the two? Grass, a ravine, bushes? He had no idea, but refused to believe there would not be three square feet of earth in which to dig a hole.

Next he sought to discover if the place was accessible. He ran the spyglass down to the shore, seeing only thick, pulpy leaves. The slope seemed steep and very difficult to scale. Below, at the water's edge: a stony embankment; a dark interweaving of thin trunks, their roots bared; then the inapproachable lagoon, its surface marred by the scattered backs of black rocks.

"They came up the side," he thought. "A passage halfway up the slope, or over the crest. The impression of impenetrable brush is an effect of distance. On the spot, the terrain is more open than it seems."

For the moment, it was impossible for him to learn anything further. He set down the spyglass. Regaining his composure, he let only the faintest smile play across his lips.

"What have you discovered?" asked Girandole.

There was no reply.

"Did you perhaps see a goat?"

"No," answered Malestro, smiling more broadly.

"Well, what then? You have been entranced by that rock for a good while now."

"Monsieur, I believe I can assure you that a passage does exist."

"Really! And it is this crag that has told you so?"

"Maybe…Do you see the profile of a monkey in it?"

Girandole studied the promontory.

"No."

"What? Look at it closely: the muzzle, the hollow about the eye. He is turned toward the southeast."

The first mate saw only a block of stone. Malestro appealed to Coridan, who was of the same opinion, and then to the rest of the crew, who were just as blind.

"Monsieur," observed Girandole, "I believe the sun has addled your brain. This boulder is but a large, shapeless mass. However, no matter! I would willingly hear out your reasoning."

"Go to the devil!" snarled Malestro, ending the discussion by turning away to contemplate the passing shore.

*

Moving along the coastline, they soon lost sight of the ship. For a long time they rowed past a dark and thickly wooded slope edged with mangroves. The forest carpeted the hillocks, folds, and indentations, sweeping over the hilltops and down again into invisible valleys. There was the murmur of birdsong, punctuated by the dry, nasal squawking of parrots. They saw the silent spectacle—for there was still the sea crashing upon the reef and the splashing of the oars—of a milky stream pouring out upon the sand between the thronging roots of two large mangroves. At that moment, every single man longed to leap into the water and brave the coral harrow to go drink that milk.

Next they encountered a tumble of debris from a huge cliff jutting out into the waves. Hulking black rocks, some lying treacherously just beneath the surface, forced them to stand out to sea. It was about eleven o'clock. Girandole decided to take a sounding and drop anchor so that the men might rest while they ate.

The lead found bottom only at a depth of forty fathoms. When the raft was anchored, they broached the casks and slopped their meager meal into a basin. They ate with disgust, haunted by the foul odors of the ship. Still, the crew enjoyed one slight but most welcome difference: the wine was from the gentlemen's stores, and it soothed their throats with a delicious aroma of figs, reminding them of the benefits of their little escapade.

They were too busy with their meal to notice the slow drifting of the raft. It was Girandole who first realized that in pulling away from the coast, they had come into the way of a northwesterly current. A little later, they began to drag anchor. They finished eating; then Girandole ordered the anchor weighed, and the men returned to their oars to take advantage of this current.

They thus drew closer to the shore. The approach was still fraught with boulders that stuck up like the backs and crests of sea serpents. The waves broke upon them furiously in swirling clouds of white mist, as though the ocean meant to shatter these obstacles. On the rocky coast hung snarled mats of vines and bouquets of dark, coriaceous leaves, often wreathed in rainbows by the spray. Beyond lay monkey apples, and the crowns of giant trees spangled with fruit the color of daffodils. For the most part, the current followed the shoreline. They could still see the promontory, while each stroke showed them more of the coast ahead. The bluffs were higher now, with steep brown cliffs where only grass and mosses grew, and little tufts of raggedy leaves. Here and there were holes into which seabirds were constantly darting and then popping out again.

They discovered an islet. It was a cable's length from shore, a mound covered in low-lying silvery vegetation. The cliff face opposite curved sharply in to form a bay. At first they could see nothing between this recess and the islet but a mass of coral rock throwing up spurs in all directions. Then a black carcass appeared, battered by the waves.

They were astonished. It was a dismasted hulk, emptied out from top to bottom, a charred ribcage that had settled and wedged between two massive boulders. Unnerved by this uncanny apparition, the men had suddenly felt the hovering presence of ghosts.

"My friends," said Girandole, "This may well be the explanation for Mavel's goat."

"This smacks more of gold than goats!" thought Malestro.

The raft drew closer. All thought the wreck was that of a brigantine. The way in to her from the sea appeared clear, and it seemed as if her company had tried to enter that rudimentary channel and then paid for their temerity by running aground.

The bay resembled the narrow neck of a goblet, in which a tongue of the sea was compressed between sheer walls hung with shadowy foliage. The corner where the walls met at the far end was lashed with foam, and disappeared quite high up among some vines.

Seeking to escape the current, which passed to seaward of the small island, Girandole turned the raft to port and stood in for the islet. His intention was to land there, study the bay, and consider how best to explore it. He had to abandon his plan, however, for the islet was surrounded by murderous rocks, all awash among waves made even more lively by these crowded shoals. Girandole realized that the only way to approach the bay was along the passage taken by the unfortunate brigantine. With Malestro urging him on, he finally agreed to attempt it.

The raft entered the channel and was immediately seized by the underset. The sea heaved angrily in a hidden tumult of crosscurrents. Sounding, they found a depth of twenty fathoms. There seemed to be a passage, after all. Judging from the rocks visible at the surface on either side, it was at best eight or ten toises wide—that is, without counting any bottlenecks or unexpected shallows that might crop up.

They proceeded very cautiously, Girandole standing at the bow, Malestro and Coridan behind him on either side. Constantly fighting the ebb and flow, heaved left and right, often borne backward, they managed to reach the wreck and throw out their grapnel.

It was neither time nor the sea that had ruined the brigantine, but fire. Only her enormous oaken ribs remained, seared and gnawed as if by massive jaws.

Coridan was sent to board her. Half the carcass was submerged. He could hoist himself upon her only by clinging to her timbers with his arms and legs. In this way he climbed to what was left of the gunwale, and was then able to see that the fairway continued on into the bay.

There did in fact appear to be a corridor through the reefs where the water, although quite turbulent for a short distance, then ran more smoothly, free of rocks and stirred only by the tide and undertow, until it reached the entrance to the goblet's neck. The breach then widened to thirty toises across, narrowing progressively between the two escarpments until these joined at an angle, where Coridan could see some sort of fault, hidden in its upper part by vines. This fault was within pistol range. From the top of the scarp on the right fell a tiny stream, cascading down to strike a ledge and vanish in a fine spray. The walls were vertical and smooth. Only at a height of five or six toises had some damp grasses and garlands of glossy foliage gained a foothold in a few scattered niches. Above, the sheer drop was broken by narrow shelves and goat paths, where ferns, palms, and clusters of fleshy leaves clung tenaciously.

Despite the efforts of the rowers, the raft was constantly buffeted by eddies, and now a sudden swell heaved it against the wreck, snapping the blade of an oar. Their situation was dangerous. Girandole called back Coridan, who scrambled down as swiftly as he could and leaped onto the raft. They disengaged the grapnel and hurried to leave the channel.

After all, they had seen enough: this opening was merely an inlet without issue, and the walls were impregnable. There was nothing to be gained there, except perhaps a bit of water, and not even that was certain. Of course, the bosun's mate might have attempted to swim into the small bay, but what then? He would have gone around in circles like a fish in a pail, and gape as he might, would have gained nothing from the waterfall beyond a splash of drizzle and much frustration. The men refused to believe they would not find a real passage farther along, even though the wreck seemed to show that those aboard had tried to force their way into this place. One mystery remained, which Girandole and his men did not dwell upon: Were these the sailors who landed the goats upon the island, or had they lost their way and come here seeking a haven?

Rounding the islet, they continued their coasting. They found the current once more, but as it pulled too far out to sea, they soon returned to hug the shore. It was then that they noticed the raft was listing. Girandole quickly discovered that two of the four large barrels on the port side had been damaged in the collision with the wreck and were taking on water. He decided to cut them loose.

It was a difficult operation. They could easily sever the ropes that held the barrels, but next they had to move one of these floats over from the other side and then rearrange them to balance the raft.

The sea greatly complicated what would have been child's play on dry land. Coridan had jumped into the water, but after much effort he realized he could not shift the barrels without help. It was Malestro who joined him in the waves, after taking off his wig, boots, and pistol. And that was how they found out he could swim.

Even then, the repairs took two hours to complete. When they got under way again, the sky was turning yellow with the approach of dusk. They passed endless cliffs topped with pale barrens and groves of monkey-apple trees, followed by forest-shrouded hills. At fifty fathoms, Girandole found a bottom of coral and shells. They cast anchor, and then some fishing lines, catching a parrot fish half an hour later that made a tasty addition to their supper, even though each man received only two mouthfuls of it, and that raw.

Night fell, and they lay down to sleep, leaving the lines in the water. The day's rowing had fatigued them all, but the weariest man among them, even though he had never touched an oar, was Coridan, whose breathing was labored and who was long kept awake by itching and aching in his limbs.

At dawn, they found two red mullet and a small catfish on their hooks. Although the fishing there was hardly splendid, it was still better than around the *flûte,* where they had never caught more than a few miserable little creatures. They breakfasted. Then the raft resumed its progress after the sun had risen near the brow of a cliff.

They made their way past a rugged shore defended by rocks ceaselessly pounded by the surf. There was nothing but ramparts and a rough sea. A tedious morning wore on, spent rowing along this forbidding coast. Their sullen thoughts sought refuge in dreams. They cherished the hope of seeing a sweetly rounded hill, a stretch of sand lapped by syrupy, violet waves, a frieze of palms in the sunlight, an open bay bordered by fields and orchards, with a river at its head to freshen the jade-green waters, a plain and natural harbor like so many others they had found during their voyage. They remembered the times they had ridden at anchor in those emerald crescents, whose manna flourished even to the water's edge. Pirogues would bring them golden fruits and copper-skinned women. They would wander through shady, perfumed groves; they drank from streams; they savored sweet pulps, plump fish, and roots with the taste of chestnuts; they devoured the nutmeg skin of girls who gave themselves for nothing—for fun or for a carpenter's nail—girls whose mouths had the fresh pinkness of seashells.

All that was elsewhere. Here, the only inhabitants were birds. They were searching for a harbor amid the defenses of a fortress. Their eyes drank deeply of shade, fruits, cool water, but their bodies were parched with longing.

They ate their midday meal in silence. They had caught no fish, and the sun beating down on their heads had exhausted them. The sea had not grown calm, and it harried the raft incessantly. Those aboard felt secretly that nature, to whom some men ascribed a soul, was ignorant of mercy.

They set off again with this dreadful thought: their survey of the island was almost complete. Once Girandole had recognized the farthest point reached in the longboat, that would be the end of it. Whereas before they had eagerly sought to make headway, now they were most unwilling to close this circuit. They wished to husband these last stretches of coastline; even if they were impassable, they still left room for hope. And Malestro remembered what the chevalier had said in speaking of these islands: "I know only too well that distressing moment when one realizes one has seen everything there is to see."

At six o'clock, overcome by the same reluctance, Girandole brought the raft in close to shore.

"Damnation!" he cried. "Can we not find a passage for a tub only ten feet wide?"

They were abeam of the southern bluff, a densely forested slope sliced off at the cliff as though by a butcher's cleaver. To the far right, the cliff face formed a spur that concealed the coast beyond. The breakers crashed upon a solid wall of coral. It was this obstacle the first mate decided to examine more closely.

They approached to within a distance of six toises and could go no farther. The waves boiled in all directions, hurling themselves against the coral rock. The men could guess what pikes, horns, and monstrous flowers of stone lay beneath the seething surface, protecting this barrier. The raft crawled along beside it.

"Monsieur Coridan," said Girandole. "What if you should attempt to get a footing there?"

The bosun's mate started. "Impossible, sir! With this sea, I'd be cut to ribbons. And that coral, it's swarming with horrid things!"

"And if there were a breach? Confound it! This raft is perhaps too large, but there should be a passage big enough for a man, after all!"

"Certainly, sir, but if someone got through, where would you have him go?"

Indeed, if Coridan had managed to cross the barrier,

he would only have been dashed against the foot of the cliffs, which streamed with water after every whiplash from the waves. The spot was ill-chosen for seeking an opening.

"Monsieur Coridan is fussing too much," said Malestro calmly. "Until now, we have been simply skirting the coast, seeking a harbor. At present it is clear that we shall find none. We must therefore cross this talus. I see no real impediment. We need only come alongside, toss out the grapnel, and leap atop it."

"And who is to do this?" asked Coridan.

"Have no fear. I will do it myself—and show you that a man may arrive upon this coral safe and sound."

"And then?" asked Girandole.

"What?"

"And then?" insisted the first mate. "Once on this talus, how will you proceed?"

"Ah, alas! I must proceed alone. This raft is too heavy to cross to the other side. We should have to take it apart, and I do not see how we could. No, I would then swim to a place where I could go ashore. There are coves over there where I see small pebble beaches. It would be surprising if…"

"Monsieur Malestro," said the first mate curtly, "I believe you must be mad. But even if, by some miracle, you should manage to do as you say, I do not see the point of it. Understand me, monsieur: the mission of this party is not to afford its members the opportunity to save their own lives."

"You are right," replied Malestro insolently. "Better for us all to come to grief together and perish with the others. Besides, it would be foolish to cross the barrier here. The same rocks lie before the ship, where they present the advantage of protecting a most hospitable shore bordered by fields and hills. Enough of this place—let us continue on our way, shall we?"

They rowed for quite a while along the wall of coral rocks. The sun had begun to set, flooding the cliffs with warm tones of honey and apricot. The sea was taking on its limpid clarity. Here and there along the coast were flat stretches of shingle, most of them imprisoned in crescents of the overhanging rock face, which had been worn away at the base by the waves. From a few of these stony beaches, however, abrupt little paths climbed upward to the sun-baked barrens above.

There was no breach large and safe enough for the raft. Girandole was thinking about putting back out to sea when a rower suddenly pointed ahead and shouted, "Look!"

Before them lay a cluster of reefs, about half a cable's length behind the coral wall. Lying among those humps was the overturned hull of a boat.

"Good God, Montpassé's jollyboat!" cried Girandole, who took up his spyglass and ordered the crew to keep rowing.

He examined the craft, which seemed in good condition. The shaft of an oar was still fixed in its oarlock, but the blade had disappeared. At first Girandole saw no other objects nearby. The long blue shadows on the ocher surface of the rock made observation difficult. Then he noticed a thin metal rod sticking up from a crevice. It was the barrel of a musket. He looked around again, but saw nothing else.

They drew slowly near, in respectful silence. The spirits hovering about this boat were not those of unknown sailors; these ghosts had the face and voice of their lost companions.

"Coridan, did anyone in that detachment know how to swim?"

"No, sir. There's never been but the four of us, in the ship's crew. Two died in the attack on the pinnace, a third was just carried off by scurvy. Which is to say he wasn't on the expedition. But, perhaps, Monsieur de Montpassé?…"

"No. Alas, no."

They had come up abeam of the wreck, and Girandole had the rowers lift their oars from the water.

"Gentlemen, it would be fitting to salute the memory of these men. But first, I should like to learn more. How did they get in? Did they take the boat over the barrier? The wreck seems to be lying on some stones. There may possibly still be some things inside her. I cannot tell if they might shed some light on the circumstances of this misfortune, yet I do think we must go see what we can find. Monsieur Malestro, you claimed not long ago to be able to cross this talus without mishap. Now is the time to prove it."

"Is this quite useful?"

"You balk, monsieur?"

Malestro sneered and waved his hand haughtily.

"Oh, I balk only at having to humor your whims."

"What! You call this a whim? Our elementary duty to—"

"Very well, then! Enough said. I will obey. Is that word agreeable to you?"

Malestro did not wait for a reply. He was already considering how best to tackle the affair at hand, scanning the coral crests to choose the best spot for a landing. He had the raft brought in closer, and asked Girandole to keep an eye on the bottom.

"Monsieur," he added, "you must lend me your shoes. I do not see myself walking barefoot on these stones and I should not like to spoil my boots. Moreover, they are hardly suitable."

Girandole hesitated, thinking at first that Malestro was joking. Faced with the other man's mute insistence, he complied.

The raft tossed in the eddies and was difficult to handle. They had drawn near a section of the reef barely a foot above the surface and engulfed by every wave that streamed foaming and seething across the pitted rock. At a distance of less than two toises, the raft became impossible to control. They hurled the grapnel across to the other side, where it gripped immediately.

Wearing his shirt, breeches, white stockings, and Girandole's shoes, Malestro grabbed the line and climbed down into the sea. Hanging on this way, he moved along the rope, which sometimes grew slack as the raft pitched this way and that, dropping him beneath the waves. Despite the buffeting, he held tight and managed to reach the swelling growths of coral. Suddenly, he was heaved against them and swallowed up by the sea. The others feared he was lost. He reappeared, however, gripping his line with one hand and grasping the rock with the other. A fresh wave swept him off. The next instant, he surfaced two toises away. For a moment they thought he would give up and return to the raft, but he swam back to the rocks, helped along by the waves, and this time he clung there so tightly that the surging water could not dislodge him.

Hoisting himself up, he was soon crouching upon the reef. He then crawled along very carefully on all fours until he came to a somewhat higher spot, where he stood to examine the area he intended to swim across. The men on the raft, still battling the swell, saw that his shirt was torn and soaked with blood. He continued to advance, reaching a part of the reef that was submerged. The water was now halfway up his calves. He halted, determined to dive in, and moved his foot to steady himself. It was then that he gave a terrible hoarse cry. The pain was such that he staggered and fell to one side. Then, half drowned, he grabbed his ankle and began screaming again.

It took a moment for those on the raft to understand and react. Girandole cut the grapnel rope and ordered the rowers to pull toward Malestro.

"Coridan," he shouted, "you must go rescue him!"

The bosun's mate was horrified.

"D'you want the same thing to happen to me?" he shouted back.

"Throw him a line, then, and you there, bring us in as close as you can! Malestro, do you think you can get back to us?"

The stricken man did not reply. He was gasping in agony, washed by the turbulent waves. The raft drew closer. A rope was tossed, but he did not take hold of it.

"Grab on to the line!" cried Girandole.

They tried again; he did not move.

"By all the saints, Malestro, get a grip on yourself, if only for one instant!"

They tried once more, and this time he found the strength to seize the rope and let himself be pulled away. He sank out of sight; they could only feel his weight on the end of the line. He did not come to the surface again until he was close to the raft. They dragged him hastily from the water and stretched him out on the platform.

"To your oars! Stand out to sea!" shouted the first mate.

He bent over Malestro, who vomited in great spasms before abruptly fainting.

They anchored at a cable's length from the reef and set out their fishing lines. Twilight had spread in turquoise and Prussian blue across the sky. The mauve-colored sea was streaked with cream. Malestro had regained consciousness. He was feverish. His torso was covered with gashes. His entire leg ached, and his ankle was enormously swollen, but he had recovered a bit of his arrogance and had demanded wine for himself and everyone else. Shortly afterward, he proposed that they drink up the rest of their supply. Ordinarily, Girandole would have refused categorically, but now he consented.

That evening, they paid their respects to Montpassé and his men. Then they spoke of the wreck of the jollyboat, for which they could find only inadequate explanations, and of Malestro's disastrous encounter with some venomous creature. Coridan saw in this accident a justification of his profound distrust of coral, and they told several grim tales that soon had the reef swarming with poisons and evil spells. Then they fell silent, overtaken by melancholy. Lassitude and the wine had their effect. It was one of those evenings when one sighs deeply, a prey to indefinable longing, and the body aspires to vast and secret and rapturous excitements. It was one of those evenings when one eagerly becomes intoxicated, when spirits expand the boundaries of the mind.

By nightfall, beneath the shimmering stars, all their suffering was drowned in a sticky, drunken slumber.

Dawn found the men gloomy and Malestro in a raging fever. The raft resumed its course without more than two words being spoken. They doubled the spur, and the shores that had been hidden from sight came into view. First they saw the far end of the barrier reefs, and then an islet Girandole recognized at once from his previous expedition. Their last hope lay in the section of coastline that was slowly being revealed. They found only cliffs, an impregnable wall stretching all the way from the spur and defended even further by black jagged rocks pounded by breakers. It was over.

The raft passed to seaward of the islet, then pulled for the spit of reefs where the *flûte* lay at anchor. They soon saw her, prostrate in the light, her wood the color of straw, her masts and yards like a tangle of willow branches. There was no sign of life. Not long afterward, a stream of smoke burst from a gunport, and they heard the cannon roar.

Chapter

X.

THE MEN ON THE RAFT felt the air thicken. It was now a hot, bitter, cottony substance of increasingly evil odor. As they approached the ship, which lay as stark and stiff as a dead tree, still bathed in a bone-yellow light, they could see the pale, stony colors of her sunbleached planking. Some of her crew were coming to the rails. Others climbed up into the shrouds. All those frail, dusty forms, as faded as figures in an ancient fresco, moved with the sullen slowness of caged animals. No one spoke or called out. They waited solemnly.

There was silence on the raft as well as it glided through the filth surrounding the vessel. Then they were alongside. They met their shipmates' gaze...The message was clear.

With grave care, two sailors lifted Malestro and hoisted him up the side ladder. Then the others followed, one by one.

When he reached the deck, Girandole came to attention, saluting the chevalier and the captain with a nod. Then he greeted Colinet, whose face was the very picture of woe. Girandole was struck by Bloche's exhausted appearance. His flabby flesh was melting away. His jabot was untied, his waistcoat unbuttoned, his boots dusty, and the seat of his breeches was dirty. He seemed to suffer from the heat, yet his skin was as dry as parchment. As for Du Mouchet, who was in shirtsleeves, his cheeks were hollow and there were dark rings under his eyes, which gleamed with a strangely savage light. He held an extinguished cigar in his hand, rolling it back and forth between his fingers.

Girandole looked quickly around him. He saw the gathering of wan wraiths, with their drawn, leathery faces, the deck in a state of neglect, and lying nearby, the pallid shape of a shrouded body. He did not remember leaving behind such utter desolation. He turned back to the captain.

"Monsieur Malestro was wounded by some venomous creature. Monsieur Saint-Foin should be summoned."

This was not necessary. The surgeon had appeared in the waist, wiping his hands with a dirty towel. His step slowed as he read upon all faces the failure of the expedition.

"Dear God," he murmured.

He climbed up the ladder and saw Malestro lying on the deck, grimacing with pain and fever, his head jerking backward with each stabbing twinge in his leg. All his arrogance had shrunk to a mute, suppressed fury.

"What happened?" asked Saint-Foin, bending over him.

"He was stung upon the ankle," replied the first mate. "A fish, it was, from what little he saw of it. This happened yesterday evening, on the coral rocks."

Saint-Foin examined the ankle, which was all one enormous red swelling, and winced.

"Did you lance the wound?"

"No."

"Did he vomit?"

"Yes, and then lost consciousness."

Saint-Foin stood up.

"My friend," he said to Malestro, "you have a tough hide. By all rights you should be dead."

"I already am," came the feeble reply.

"No jests, please. You are not out of danger yet. Take him to his cabin. Carry him gently—you must not stir up his blood."

Four men maneuvered him carefully down the ladder. Before following his patient, Saint-Foin fixed his tired, drooping gaze upon Girandole.

"You could not get through, then?"

The first mate shook his head.

"Dear God," the surgeon murmured once again.

But his nose had twitched. He turned toward the place where the dead man lay, sewn up in sailcloth. His burial had been interrupted by the raft's return. Six paces away, Saint-Foin smelled the corpse's hideous, sweetish stench.

"Captain," he said, "we should not keep this man any longer."

"Yes," said Bloche, taking a moment to pull himself together. "Colinet! Have the raft unloaded. Then we will proceed with the ceremony. As for you, Girandole, pray go along and refresh yourself—if you can...This old tub is as hot and dry as a smoking coal. Wait upon me in the great cabin, where you will make your report."

There had been an increase in deaths over the past two days: three the day before last, one the following night, four the next day, and the latest toward the end of that very morning. The sun blazed away ever more fiercely. Those on the raft had not been so severely affected, but in the torrid bowels of the ship, the men had suffered terribly. This heat hastened the last agony of the sick, and their corpses decomposed with frightening speed. They were quickly got rid of, but they left behind a pervasive presence that no amount of vinegar could erase, like ghosts waiting to welcome the next body brought up from the between-decks.

As it was, there were now as many bedridden souls in the seamen's berth as there were in the sick bay, which made twice the work for Saint-Foin and Robinot. The surgeon usually chose to take care of those below, thus escaping the worst of it, but he could not avoid the sick bay altogether. He had to attend the most serious cases or simply send Robinot below in his place when his assistant's grumbling passed all bounds. Saint-Foin had grown very weak and was still tormented by the nauseating odors that sometimes made him run to vomit through a porthole. He was also worried about the acute abdominal pain that constantly returned to plague him and which no remedy could relieve.

As for Robinot, he seemed indestructible. For ten days he had been wearing the same smock, which had once been white and was now gray with sweat and grime and spotted with crusty dried blood. When Saint-Foin upbraided him for this, he replied gruffly that one doesn't muck out stables in silks and satins.

In the sick bay, Robinot's temper was equable—that is to say, always surly. He made no bones about wiping anyone's nose, bossing about even the brawniest hands. Indeed, it was with them that he would carry on the most outrageously, as though piqued by the challenge. Over a trifle, he would suddenly begin to curse and insult them, leaving his victims too stunned to respond with a punch in his foul mouth. They had grown used to him. These rude insults were part and parcel of the fellow, and it would never have occurred to anyone to take offense at his "Move your moldy carcass" or "Shift your crotty arse." He was the same way with the dying—merely busier, and more quiet. It was only in their last moments that he allowed himself to speak a few words of comfort. Then he could be heard murmuring, in a suddenly pater- nal voice, "Time to go, my lad. 'Tis over. Go on, I tell you, let go…" And all who had overheard that voice were ready to forgive him his worst offenses.

He did not like going down between decks, for there he was no longer at home. In the sick bay, he had his little ways, his special places for his compounds and electuaries;

he put away the linens, washed the buckets, threw out the lint, moving about according to a schedule he alone understood. On that point he was quite fussy, and never failed to reprove Saint-Foin for the slightest disruption in his routine. The surgeon usually let him have his say, but every once in a while, exasperated, he would send him below.

There, surly Robinot became downright bad-tempered. Without a word, he would descend the ladder with his instruments and enter the screened-off space where the crew slept, immediately making a show of distaste for all he saw and smelled, casting glances of disgust on all sides. "Filthy swine!" he always snapped, which disconcerted the men no end, since they knew what a hell the sick bay was. Then he would go over to the first hammock, briefly examine the patient, peer into his mouth like a horse dealer, palpate his salivary glands, and set about bleeding him, in silence. This mutism was peculiar to his visits between decks. When a patient told him about his new aches and pains, Robinot would pretend not to hear. One had to go on at some length before he would reply.

"What d'you expect?" he would say. "You're rotting like the rest of 'em. You started rotting on the day you was born. Scurvy just speeds you along. This bit goes to pot here, another gives way there...'Tis the natural order of things: 'tis your dunghill cooking away."

One day, a sailor within earshot complained.

"D'you have to lay out all that shit?" he protested. "That's not what the man asked of you."

Robinot whirled around.

"What shit?" he cried. "And who's laying it out if it ain't you, you great crotty arse? You stink like a heap of dead cats and you want us all to smell roses? Just wait. Is it yourself you're trying to fool, you rotter? Have you got as much crap in your head as in your butt? You think like an ostrich—you imagine 'tis enough to close your eyes and bung up your nostrils for nothing to happen. Listen hard, you dunce: you pretend till you're blue in the face, you'll not keep from turning into a fine piece of stinking offal we'll heave straight overboard."

The man did not break Robinot into little pieces. He took his tongue-lashing without a word. He sensed vaguely, but enough to hang fire, that what was grinding him down so cruelly was the sickness itself, and not this foul-mouthed little fury who was trying, after all, to save him.

After the return of the raft, Saint-Foin had been busy seeing to Malestro, so Robinot had had to go down between decks once again. Surprisingly, the failure of the expedition had not worsened his temper. On the contrary, he seemed less cross than usual.

He found the men gathered around the raft's crew, plying them with questions. Some had hunkered down, holding their heads in their hands; one man was crying.

Without taking any notice of anyone—and without greeting them with his customary "Filthy swine!"— Robinot auscultated his patients, bled them, administered Venice treacle, applied green powder, examined a plaster, and paused at the side of the Iroquois, who was far gone, and whose body was almost entirely covered with blue-black discolorations. Robinot still had three or four hammocks to visit when he saw a sick man arise from one of them. He was about to call out that this was not the moment to wander off, but the man was simply going to his sea chest, so Robinot watched him out of the corner of his eye. It was a topman named Brousseau, a short, sturdy fellow with sandy hair whose milky, densely freckled skin had never learned to tan. His torso, as rosy and lean as a cut of veal, was now studded with tubercles. From his sea chest he removed a small knife, a medallion, a thin chain, and a knotted handkerchief, which he untied so that he might verify its contents. Then he stuffed everything into his pockets, closed the chest, and headed toward the ladder to the waist.

"Where are you off to with your things?"

The topman did not hear him, or did not want to hear.

"Ahoy, Brousseau, where are you going?"

The man turned his back to him and faced the ladder. Robinot realized that he was off his head. He strode up to him and grabbed his arm. Brousseau gave him a sidelong glance, a look that immediately turned mean. Then he jerked his arm away, and as he did so, spittle flew from his mouth.

"Poor bastard!" exclaimed Robinot. "'Tis not enough that your guts are rotting—now you've gone soft in the headpiece."

With surprising strength, the man lifted a foot and

planted it squarely on Robinot's chest, sending him flying a good four paces away.

Everyone looked up, but without understanding what was happening.

"Catch him!" shouted Robinot, still lying flat on his back. "He's going to jump overboard!"

The other man had fled. Three of his shipmates rushed up the ladder. When they piled out into the waist, the fugitive was approaching the steps. They made a dash for him. He had stumbled right in front of the gangway and was getting to his feet. The closest of his pursuers managed to seize his ankle. The sick man kicked at him, but it was too late. The others had nabbed him.

He struggled for only a moment, then let them carry him away. He was frothing at the mouth, as though with hydrophobia. As they took him below, his captors asked what had gotten into him. He did not reply. Down between decks, when everyone had gathered around to question him, he remained silent. Robinot, back on his feet again, did not intervene. He let the men talk. Bat-la-lame tried to show the poor fellow how insane his action had been.

"After all, Brousseau, you can't swim! You'd wind up with your gob crawling with crabs. And where would you wind up? Knocking on a wall of poison coral. You heard what your shipmates said. Malestro nearly croaked there. Never tell me you wanted to end it all! Speak up, you poor bugger, what did you want?"

There was a wild look in Brousseau's eyes. He seemed a thousand miles away. From time to time, he darted a glance at the ladder, then looked back at his companions, as though waiting for them to stop pestering him. Perhaps he eventually understood that they would keep bothering him until he gave them an answer, for he finally spoke up, in a voice clotted with spittle.

"I want to drink goat's milk."

Everyone was perplexed at this, except Robinot.

"The swine's delirious," he said. "He'll have to be kept under guard, or he'll bugger off again the first chance he gets."

"What d'you mean by that, keeping him 'under guard'?" asked Bat-la-lame.

"The same as what Bloche and Saint-Foin would mean."

"You'd shut him up in the hold? And him with scurvy?"

"Ah, just you do the shutting up, you bonehead! Is it my fault that you're all crumbling away like frozen timber? And that this bastard's lost his wits into the bargain? Well, then! 'Tis your own affair, after all. Let him drown hisself, if you like. 'Twill be one less carcass for me to deal with. But you be sure of this: I mean to inform Saint-Foin as soon as I've finished in this shit-pit of yours."

Soon afterward, as they sat at dinner in the great cabin, Girandole told the others about the ring of coral and the cliffs, the remains of the brigantine blocking the passage, the discovery of the jollyboat, and Malestro's accident on the coral.

They listened, and went back over certain details, trying to understand. Their thoughts were racing ahead as the first mate spoke. So, there was no chance of finding a harbor. They would have to steel themselves and attempt desperately to break through...or await the wind. But this wind, what good was it to them now? This wind so hopelessly absent since they first sighted the island, this wind that had withdrawn like a discreet servant, that sprang up only to do them ill, that seemed to prevent them from landing as well as from leaving...Yes, of what use would it be now, except to sail for Caine only to die along the way?

Bloche sat gloomily, his chin sunk upon a puffy necklace of flesh. He had left a drop of soup in his dish, which he contemplated in silence, his hands resting on the arms of his chair. Across the table, the chevalier observed him nervously.

"Captain," he said, "this island is defending herself, yes! But we must have her. If she will not yield gracefully, then let us force her."

Bloche looked up at him wearily, almost contemptuously.

"And how would you do this, pray? Would you have us drive the ship upon the reef?"

"If the wind comes up, that is what we should do."

"A pretty picture. The ship is staved in, and we cannot repair her hull. So tell me, monsieur, how you mean to get away from this accursed island."

"My sole concern is to get to her. I do not care a damn about leaving her."

Trinquet peered at the chevalier with his badly swollen eyes.

"I see, Jacques, that those demons have got you again."

"What demons, Cornelius?" protested the chevalier. "This isle is beautiful and will save us!"

"You've lost your heart like that many times before."

"I was mistaken. This one..."

He fell abruptly silent, as though overwhelmed by something inexpressible.

The others now considered less radical means of landing on the island. The main thing, in Girandole's opinion, was to establish a link between the sea and the shore. Since the raft was too heavy to cross the barrier, they should build another, lighter one they could pass over the reef, and which would then ply back and forth in the lagoon.

This solution seemed appropriate. Still, they would have to transport this second raft, which meant that men would have to climb up on the reef. Bloche doubted there would be a rush of volunteers.

"In that case, I will go!" exclaimed the chevalier.

The captain was astonished.

"You, monsieur? Do you at least know how to swim?"

"No."

"It is most dangerous, I warn you."

"So I have gathered."

Bloche hesitated, and consulted his first mate with a glance before replying.

"Very well, then! But you must take three men with you."

"Allow me to propose myself," said Saint-Foin, with unwonted military crispness.

Bloche's smile was both ironical and affectionate.

"No, Saint-Foin. Firstly, I cannot see you, clumsy as you are, capering about on those treacherous rocks. Secondly, we have need of you here. Still, I admire your pluck."

"It is not pluck, Captain, but urgency."

"If you will. 'Tis all the same. Tell me, Girandole…"

The first mate stiffened, a reaction Bloche interpreted as one of dismay.

"Set your mind at ease: I shall not call upon you for this. Your presence on the ship is all the more valuable in that I fear I may soon prove unable to fulfil my duty."

"Captain!"

"Enough of that. Do you think Colinet would volunteer?"

"I do not know."

"I hope so. We would have to seek next among the petty officers. Which reminds me, that young assistant of Picot-Fleury's, what state is he in? I had found him to be courageous."

"He is now bedridden," said Saint-Foin.

"Well…Well, well," sighed Bloche, momentarily overcome by a swarm of dark thoughts. "So, gentlemen, we must begin building this second raft with all speed. Girandole, you will give the two carpenters their orders."

"One of them is on the sick list," said Saint-Foin.

"Ah…And the cooper, is he also in your care?"

"No. He died abruptly yesterday."

Bloche's temper got the better of him for a moment, and he almost vented his irritation on the surgeon. Then he pulled himself together.

"Girandole," he said simply, with a sudden weariness, "see to it."

Then he apologized to the others for leaving them and hauled himself out of his chair.

"Tell me, how is Malestro doing?" he asked Saint-Foin.

"He is tough, astonishingly so. I think he will pull through."

"Well, Saint-Foin," remarked Bloche as he left the cabin, "that is truly the first good news you have brought me in ages."

Toward the end of the afternoon, there were two deaths, one right after the other. One of them occurred between decks. This was the first time the men had witnessed the last moments of a scorbutic. It was the Iroquois. He could not be shifted, for he choked at the slightest movement, and Saint-Foin had to resign himself to leaving him where he lay. He was covered with sores whose livid, spongy flesh bled at the touch; his purplish and peeling gums were so swollen that his lips were quite curled back. Gaping under his eagle nose, this mummy's mouth drooled constantly, slavering on a chin as gray and raspy as a millstone. Without moving, he had begun to rattle in the back of his throat, and blood had trickled from his nose and mouth, slowly welling up until his throat was clogged. Stiff, unmoving, he died like that, with his jaw straining open as though he were a dog about to bite.

This agony shocked them all, the sailor who dashed to a porthole no less than those transfixed with anguish at the sight of the corpse. A confused mixture of terror and repugnance spread among them, and many fled. Up on deck they found the other dead man, who had been hastily removed from the sick bay. They understood that there was no longer any escape from this death now prowling throughout the ship.

When night fell, all those who found the strength to leave their hammocks and come up on deck to sleep could smell—below, all around, and within themselves—the inexorable workings of decay. These men, so used to their own musky odor, their foul breath, their vomiting and flatulence, the musty stink of their underclothes, the violent stench of their excrement, and all their bestial fetor, now discovered how the business of death could draw from a body smells of unimaginable pestilence.

At eleven o'clock, a sailor who had been assigned to the gentlemen's service, replacing a servant who had fallen ill, finished his duties and joined his mates resting on the forecastle. As he advanced through their midst, he heard low groans and panting breath, but even more unsettling were the men who lay with their eyes wide open, wrapped in a spectral, monumental silence. No one paid any attention to the new arrival, who leaned back against the ship's bow, fishing a cutty and a pigskin tobacco pouch from his pocket. He calmly packed the clay bowl, brought out a tinderbox, and struck a light. He drew the first puff on his pipe with a kind of weary sensuality.

"Coridan's gone on the sick list," he announced.

No one turned a hair. They had heard the remark but could think of nothing to say in reply. The sailor continued to smoke for a moment, gazing at the moon rising in the sky. He listened, through the rustling of the sea, to the endless cooing on the island. From the sleepy herd on deck came a lone voice.

"And Malestro, is he done for?"

"Seems as he ain't," replied the sailor.

An occasional moan floated up from the sick bay. A stifling torpor seemed to weigh these cries down and snuff them out. The wailing would stop. Silence would return, heavy with the expectation of another groan.

The sailor drew on his pipe at long intervals, but often enough to keep it alight. He smoked for some time, with practiced skill.

"Bloche keeled over at the end of supper."

He could tell from the slight catch in everyone's breath that he had hooked his audience. He was more than willing to elaborate, drawing out the pause between each sentence.

"They carried him to his cabin. I helped. He's damned heavy, that man. Saint-Foin bled him. After that, he felt better. The others came to see him. I saw my chance and tossed off his glass of sweet wine."

XI.

LANTERN IN HAND, the chevalier was roaming through the dark desolation of the storerooms. Why, on that morning, had he gone down into the belly of the ship? He hadn't given it a thought. He had only felt the desire to go below, to open doors, to explore this territory he had disdained to visit until now.

For the last few days, he had felt pent up in his cabin. He was now much afflicted with fever, sleeping restlessly, beset with confused dreams that roused his senses, leaving him to awaken, boiling and greedy for air. Even though he had eaten the same diet as his companions, he had not been greatly affected by scurvy, aside from some aching in his gums. But he suffered as they all did from hunger and thirst. One dream returned night after night: he was bodily entering an enormous, succulent fruit, drowning in its pulp, kneading it, biting into it hungrily, feasting on its juicy flesh, even enjoying the feel of

it on his own skin. Perhaps it was to escape these voluptuous obsessions that he no longer stayed in his cabin.
Perhaps he was trying to shake them off that morning,
down in the stinking, shadowy hold that Bloche had
declared strictly off-limits for most of the crew.

He was alone. He passed large blind compartments
where barrels, butts, and impressive casks were piled
clear up to the thick deck beams. He wandered haphazardly, turning here or there, retracing his steps to go off
in a different direction. The sour-smelling coat of pitch
everywhere could not mask the odors of mold and stagnant water. He surveyed all these casks, which seemed
abandoned. When he rapped them with his knuckles they
rang hollow. He did not find one that was full.

And yet these huge storerooms, he remembered, had
been stocked with an abundant larder. A royal profusion
of wine, fresh water, vegetables, salt meats, cod and herring, cheese, flour, sugar, biscuit, all augmented by the
poultry, pigs, sheep, oxen, and goats penned in the waist.
What a handsome vessel of provisions she had been then,
with her air of slightly matronly nobility! A noble resi-
dence and a floating farm: a château gone voyaging with
its outbuildings.

"This *flûte* seemed victualed for a trip around the
globe," mused the chevalier. "One ocean voyage was
enough. Nothing so trying as sailing the high seas. It
wears you down, wears you out. The sea is nothing but
salt. A single horizon and some salt. And all you do there
is look out for land. You burn your eyes away with look-

ing and addle your brains. It eats up everything: provisions, body and soul."

Now the rancid air smelled sharper, laced with a strong aroma of leeks. When he touched the planking, a warm, sticky substance with a spicy odor came away on his fingers. He was bedeviled by gnats drawn to the light and his sweat. One of them blundered into his eye, and he had to rub his sore eyelid to get rid of the insect.

He looked into a series of shot lockers containing cannonballs and cartridge bags packed with gunpowder. Those stores had hardly been used at all, and the chevalier—forgetting the excellent wine from Caine— reflected that they were truly the only ones not to have spoiled. They had fired off shot only twice. The first time to save Malestro and his two confederates, paddling away in a bought or stolen canoe and closely pursued by howling warriors. The second time had been that accursed day when the crew of the pinnace were massacred.

He retraced his steps, or at least tried to, for the passages were short and interconnected, and they led him every which way. He did not mind.

The wood all about him creaked constantly, so that he sometimes thought he heard approaching footsteps. He also heard at intervals, in the distance, the grinding of an enormous cask, screeching like a cart axle shifted by an impatient horse. He encountered no one, and saw no sign that either stewards or carpenters were at work anywhere. The shadows were inhabited, however. Faint noises, pattering, and sudden scrabbling betrayed the presence of rats. They were everywhere, and sometimes the lantern illuminated a round back trotting away, muscles rippling beneath the fur. They were not frightened; they were simply showing a rather contemptuous prudence. Some of them even turned to face the intruder before darting off, their eyes glowing red in the light. This boldness irritated the chevalier, who regretted having come below decks unarmed.

Gradually, he grew used to their company, and was soon completely absorbed in his thoughts again. He reflected that he had not come down into the belly of the ship more than twice, and never alone. Not from indifference, but on the contrary, so that he might keep beneath him vast unexplored spaces. He was saving these discoveries. He knew that if the quarterdeck, the forecastle, the entire upper deck became too confining, he would still be able to escape into these territories. The day had arrived, and he paced through the forbidding darkness in an effort to amuse himself.

It was not easy. Aside from the austerity of the place, he had to contend with his own impatient nature, so quick to turn indifferent, which had put paid to many an island in the course of the voyage. That was how he was: the pleasure he took in penetrating into the unknown was equaled by the speed with which he tired of it. Boredom grew with familiarity. From encounter to encounter, from discovery to conquest, this failing had led him astray in the end. At first he had longed only to find a shady tree and lie down beneath it for a thousand years, but gradually he had sought to stave off this lassitude with more tortuous mysteries. It was no longer enough for him that an island be a little world, unique and full of grace; he required charms both savage and refined. He had been drawn to strange pleasures, he had coveted dark islands, developed a taste for mazy foliage, musky perfumes, sultriness, lush riots of plant life. What he sought in these depths was no longer delight, but a dizzying amazement—of which he tired in turn, and which left him steeped not in boredom but in revulsion. This wandering had led him to an island ringed with salt marshes, from which sprang a forest of tall trees drenched in mist, a tangle of vines and naked roots, bathed in the heady, viscous, deadly scent of giant decomposing flowers. There he had found impure animal pleasures. That was the last island to enthrall him. He had fled in such a state of disgust that he had believed himself forever drained of this longing. It was only his desire for these corruptions that had passed, and now his senses were awakening again, inflamed by this island gorged on light. He dreamed of endless bliss.

"Why am I so sure of this island?" he wondered. "What do I know of her, save that she is locked up like an oyster? Why this certainty, then? Is it not because I do not have her and am kept from having her?"

This fine bout of self-criticism was enough for him, proving as it did that he was neither blinded by desire nor deranged by thirst. He swiftly brushed all these doubts aside.

He climbed up some short ladders and down some

more; one of them brought him to the sail locker. Thick pads of bleached and unbleached hemp lay piled up there, along with the ship's spare suits of sails, including whole topsails with cringles worked into their bolt ropes. There were pieces of uncut sailcloth, and the old canvas used to make the sailors' shrouds. An ell of canvas lay spread out upon the floor, as if waiting to be cut.

The chevalier was moving toward a door when he saw two green eyes light up and leap from among the heaps of material. Thinking the creature was jumping out at him, he jumped back himself, protecting his head with his arm. For an instant he was stunned by a burst of light at the base of his skull. The thing had not attacked him. It was now running and bounding crazily upon the cloth bundles. It was a scrawny tiger cat, possessed by some inexplicable terror that drove it to ricochet all around the room rather than escape up the ladder. The chevalier took a deep breath to calm his racing heart.

"This cat has gone mad," he thought, "and I am not the cause of its fright, or it would have fled from here..."

Observing its strange frenzy, he noticed at last that the animal was missing an ear and half of its tail. He thought of the rats, capable of banding together to attack a cat and tear it to pieces.

"'Tis more than likely it wishes to remain in here, rather than risk its neck out in that death trap. The rats have been tormenting it. Judging from those missing pieces, it has felt their teeth. Monstrous vermin! They have driven it insane..."

The door opened onto a gallery set halfway up the side of the lions' den. The enormous cable of the sheet anchor filled the entire tier. There was still enough space, however, in which to confine a handful of prisoners. No one was there now. The one-eyed sailor had been released. The only traces of his presence were a wooden basin and a vague odor of excrement that blended with the muddy fetor of the room.

The chevalier walked along the gallery, rejoined the central passage, and went to try the doors on the other side. Certain among them were locked, probably to safeguard some pitiful last stores of provisions. He had grown calm again, and now began to see the dark belly of the ship as a kind of cellar. He had not expected such a dismal tour.

"What good are all these doors," he wondered, "if they lead only to shadows? 'Tis a tomb with drawers, and I do not much care for it. Sordid, and too vast. I do not see myself dead and swallowed up by boundless space. The idea of decaying at the bottom of the ocean is repulsive. I want to be assured of a sturdy wooden coffin with a few feet of earth overhead. What is the point of being dead if one cannot lie down once and for all?"

He considered that he seemed unlikely to end his days on dry land.

"Ah!" he thought with a sudden pang, "isn't it the sea that awaits me, as it does all these other poor souls? With a touch more ceremony, perhaps, but all the same. Unless I prove the last to die, in my bed, alone on the drifting ship, slowly borne back by the currents to the bay of Caine. 'Twould not be the first wreck to pitch up there, and some have come directly from the devil. A simple matter of time. A corpse cares nothing for time. The drier I shall be, the less bother for my gravediggers. I shall keep on my ring, so they will know who I am. They will bury me in that crypt set apart in the middle of a pomegranate grove."

He spoke of his death but did not believe in it. He hardly believed in the deaths of his companions. He was certainly affected by their suffering and the ravages of scurvy, but he did not feel menaced by the growing danger. He merely felt quite irritable, on edge, and beset by waves of melancholy.

"I would have been laid to rest there, in that small clearing where they go to gather the fruit in season and pay their respects, in passing, to Grandfather's old bones. The sea is not far off. A rather steep mule track leads down there…"

He thought about Caine, that narrow strip of land, back in the rollicking times when he had gone larking with friends and galloping through the dusty woodlands.

"I left Caine because it was a sort of island. And I let myself fall for the first true island…"

He had gone even farther down into the ship and was prowling among rooms that seemed abandoned. There were huge pieces of dunnage wood, crusted with greasy dirt, that gave these low cells the air of an ancient, long-forgotten vault. He walked along the inward-leaning wall, which curved in more sharply as it joined the deck. He found a hatch and a ladder going down still farther.

"Where in damnation can this lead?"

Hanging the lantern into the black hole, he could make out the humped backs of large stones. He was immediately repulsed by a miasmal stink. It was the bilge. He had caught a glimpse of the stagnant water, as dark as liquid manure, in which the ballast sat. The bed of the swamp was there, a macerating brew of putrid, concentrated foulness, giving off a stench so thick and strong that he had felt as if he were drinking it.

"Ugh! The sewer in here is worse than the one outside. The ship is oozing like spoiled fruit. And this is the vile residue. I have hit bottom."

He hastened back up the ladder and wandered through passages without knowing where he was. He opened doors to rooms piled high with empty barrels or littered only with a straw pallet or a few disparate objects. He began to feel dazed by the labyrinth, the gnats, the light dancing on the blackish-brown wood, and the oppressive dampness that plugged his throat like a cork. Sometimes he saw huge cockroaches scurrying along; he crushed them underfoot. He heard only his steps on the planking and the faint creak of his boots. It astonished him not to hear any sound from the men overhead. He found this silence as painful as the groans that sometimes reached him in the night.

"The sickness works in secret. It nibbles, it gnaws... Then it touches a nerve."

He had just remembered that at dawn, a man had suddenly begun to whinny, and this torment had seemed to him to come straight up from hell.

In the end, the darkness and solitude overwhelmed him. There were as many fevers hatching down below as there were out in broad daylight. The hold was nothing more than the vile and fetid bowels of a lazaretto.

As he stepped into a small empty room that he intended to pass through, he spied, off to the right, a door with its central panel missing. Sitting on the threshold was a rat. His intrusion startled the rodent, which pattered off across a scattering of straw. He took a step, and another rat emerged from the opening to follow the first one. Then a third appeared, a fourth, and soon there was a small swarm of them. The chevalier stopped, shocked by their numbers.

He had already noticed a sweetish odor, which he took to be the stubborn trace of provisions stored there until recently. Then came the sudden and unmistakable smell of carrion. He examined the room by the light of his lantern, finding nothing but a few wisps of straw and a frayed scrap of rope. The rats had lost their momentary fear; a few still watched him from the corners of their eyes, but others were edging back toward the door. He noticed blood on one rat's snout. He felt a sudden presentiment. Forgetting his disgust, he ran to the opening.

There he received a fright that sent him staggering backward: the lantern had revealed a half-eaten corpse.

The chevalier's bones turned to ice. He fought against

a violent urge to vomit by swallowing nervously and opening his mouth to gulp in air, but this same air was filled with the sweet stench that caused his stomach to heave.

Trembling, his skin clammy with cold sweat, he struggled to control himself, torn between fascination and the desire to flee. He was still staring at the corpse.

The body was leaning against the bulkhead at the back of the tiny room, clad only in a pair of trousers, beneath which rats were busily at work. The flesh had been flayed in places, and a wound in the side exposed the viscera. The face showed only two black holes where the eyes had been, and the tattered jaw hung open in a ferocious grin, hideously exaggerated by the swollen gums. A long lock of stiff blond hair dangled from the skull.

"The cabin boy," said the chevalier in a low voice.

He recognized the slight, young limbs and the little silver medal around the neck.

There had been a crowd of rats until the chevalier's appearance in the doorway, when they dispersed, but only into the shadows. Those rooting about inside the trousers had decided to stay put, after poking their gory noses outside for a moment. Gradually, when the intruder remained motionless, a few rats slipped boldly behind the body. Others joined them. Some came out into the open to climb back onto their prey. Soon the ragged flesh was once more tufted with gray pompons and draped with ringed tails as soft as earthworms.

This impudence revolted the chevalier, who felt a furious

desire to kill the rats. He tried to think how he might do this. He had no weapon. He was enraged, almost to the point of stamping them to death. But he did not dare. Not because he feared them. It was the idea of touching the body, even with the tip of his boot sole, that appalled him.

Helpless, he turned and fled.

He could still smell the corpse and the nauseous sweet odor. He walked swiftly along, telling himself, amid the confusion of his thoughts, that this time, he had indeed touched bottom. He tramped through passages without knowing where he was going. He wanted only to get away.

He pushed open doors, crossed rooms, entered short passageways that abruptly proved dead ends. He roamed through cluttered storerooms jammed with crates, barrels, tools, and even chests packed with gifts intended for natives. It seemed so absurd to him, this wealth of showy goods sleeping in the desolate belly of the ship—not far from a dead boy.

He looked for a ladder leading upward and found only a succession of rooms and passages leading nowhere. He had turned and turned again until he grew bewildered; he had doubled back a dozen times, and a dozen times had thought he remembered passing by the same place. He was sick of this loathsome maze, of all this useless space, and of his own inability to master his revulsion.

Then the flame in the lantern began to flicker. He was following a narrow corridor lined with doors. He took a few more steps and the candle went out.

Thinking he had brought a tinderbox, he searched his pockets, but found nothing. He stood still for a moment in the pitchy darkness, feeling suddenly very tired and feverish. The sooty odor from the candlewick was overpowered by a strong scent of resin: he thought there must be a tar bucket somewhere off to his left. He made his way to a door frame, stepped over the threshold, and groped around for something he could use as a seat. He felt as though he were stirring thick, sticky ink.

He finally resigned himself to sitting in the passage, after deciding that the tar would keep the rats away. To make sure of this, he held his breath and listened intently. Now he could hear faint scratching noises, but he realized that there was nothing moving nearby. He sat down with his back against the wooden partition and tried to recover his sangfroid.

"Why did that child die here? What prevented him from going back up? Was he taken with a sudden weakness? Maybe. But he must have come down here. Alone, in secret. And he had no reason to do so. Where did he sleep? In the 'tween-decks? In the sick bay? How is it that his disappearance went unnoticed? Although it is true we are grown careless in this respect..."

In spite of all these questions, he had to admit that the cabin boy had come below for some mysterious reason, and the chevalier could not ignore the connection between this going to ground and his death.

"What morbid animal instinct was at work? A child does not abandon himself thus to the darkness..."

He felt keenly responsible for the cabin boy's death. He grimaced in anguish, then tried to throw off his gloom.

"After all! Is it my fault the wind has deserted us? Is it my fault this island rebuffs us? Is it my fault people are dying within a stone's throw of salvation?"

The corpse had shaken him. He was not familiar with death close at hand. He knew death only at a distance. He thought only of the idea of death, with many embellishments. And now death had slapped him hard, spitting horrible filth in his face, grabbing at his throat and belly. Now he had seen a long lock of blond hair hanging down over features chewed to shreds. Everything within him had changed, weakened, including this fine sturdy body that was now no more than slops. And with what little that remained of his reason, he had raged against death, prepared to commit the most awful violence, and had proved unable even to tackle a few rats...

Then he heard something pattering toward him. He jumped up and shouted, his nerves jangling.

He listened. The trotting had stopped dead, but he did not hear the sounds of a retreat. The animal was probably a few steps away, sniffing at him. He remembered the bloody muzzles of the rats he had seen upon the corpse. Once again he felt the urge to kill.

He was still feverish, but his fatigue had given way to anger. He tried to think how he might satisfy his hatred. He had to be content with stamping his heel on the deck. To his fury, the animal did not budge. He banged on the deck again, in vain.

"You stinking vulture," he screamed, "do you want me to crush you to a pulp?"

Then, as his adversary still lay low, he groped round for his lantern, seized it, and hurled it at the rat. He heard a lengthy crash of clattering metal and broken glass. That was all.

Now he was in a quandary. He supposed that the rat was perhaps long gone, but he could not manage to convince himself of this.

"Will no one ever come?" he said out loud.

He stood there for a minute, staring into the utter darkness. Then, furious at being driven away—for he felt unable to tolerate that silent, invisible presence—he set out, feeling his way blindly on.

He walked for a long time, sliding his fingers across the greasy planking. What he feared more than anything was that he might come upon the corpse again. The thought of accidentally touching it made his blood run cold. He reassured himself with the idea that the stench would surely be enough to warn him.

Finally, after endless wandering, he thought he heard footsteps. He stopped to listen: someone was coming down a ladder. He saw no gleam of light. The man had to be around a few corners and behind a bulkhead or two, for the sound of his step echoed around several obstacles.

"Hello!" shouted the chevalier.

Silence. The man must have been listening.

"Hello!" he cried again. "This way!"

After a moment, a hoarse and rather high-pitched

voice replied, from what seemed like ten leagues away.

"Who is there?"

"Chevalier Du Mouchet!"

There was another pause, and quite a long one.

"Who is it?"

"Du Mouchet! I have no light anymore…Dammit! Are you coming to get me or not?"

This sharp tone decided the man, who set out in search of the chevalier, guided by his occasional shouts of "Ho!" and "Over here!" At last the chevalier saw the halo of a lantern come whipping along the bulkheads like a flouncing yellow skirt. The sailor appeared. He was a stocky man who listed from side to side as he walked, as though he were limping with both legs. The light playing upon his face from below deformed his features grotesquely, masking his eyes with two leaves of shadow. He looked like some grim boatman from the nether world.

XII.

IT WAS DUSK. All day long there had been a racket of sun and restless, skittering waves. The sky was solid blue, dark and incandescent. The men burned their eyes on it, and soon gave up looking at that half of the world. It was the oppressive heat, like that inside a red-hot caldron from which all air had fled, that drew their faces upward to the lid. Overhead stretched nothing but a cloudless sheet of bronze. An immense vault, lowering away. It engulfed the sea, the island, the ship, and the tiny figures gathered on deck to stand praying that the skies would be rent asunder.

Big gusts of tepid wind now blew over surging billows, churning up the bottle-green depths, leaving streaks of soot, lead, silt, earth, and then suddenly, with a great sigh, the heavens gave way.

The rain had not come sweeping over the sea but had fallen from above, as though from a cistern that had overflowed—or even burst, so torrential was the downpour. At first the men were suffocated by the din and the battering deluge. Then, tingling all over, mouths gaping skyward, they caught their breath again, and came to life. The rain flooded them with joy. Some gesticulated amid the splashing; others screamed between gulped mouthfuls, so giddy they could only grunt their happiness; one kneeled, spread his arms, and lifted his ecstatic face to the blessed spattering; another scooped up water from the deck with his hands, sucking at it greedily. Finally, a few wiser heads set out pails and tubs and unfolded large pieces of canvas, holding them by the edges.

The cloudburst continued, shaken by flurries of wind. The entire vessel was streaming, and that water slipping away into the sea was more valuable than gold. Containers of all kinds were fetched: mugs, crates, clogs, hastily emptied chests, kettles, basins, jugs, casks with their tops hurriedly staved in. The petty officers, the cook, the gentlemen—everyone did his share. The chevalier was even observed bringing his two pairs of boots, while Colinet set out half a dozen tricorns, upside-down.

The rain slackened and abruptly ceased. It had drenched the ship, leaving behind a strong smell of damp wood and a splattering of pewter droplets. It also left a chalky sky and an unquiet sea. But no wind.

Twilight came on swiftly. Tearing themselves from their bliss, the men stored away the water they had collected, enough to last two days. They rejoiced to be delivered from that furnace, from the blinding glare that pierced right through to the backs of their skulls. The mild, light air had lost its stuffiness, yet the pleasant atmosphere that bathed the deck was not the work of nightfall. The weather had changed, they thought. For an hour? For a day? They had no way of knowing. But so great was their euphoria that they saw in this the beginning of good fortune.

The construction of the raft was resumed at the work site set up in the waist. They had been sawing logs there since mid-morning, and with much difficulty; the pit-sawyers, chosen from among the least enfeebled hands, possessed neither the skill nor the energy demanded. Moreover, since the planks had to be cut thin to keep the raft light, they had to be sawn from the largest logs, to ensure the necessary width and strength. The men had not finished by the end of the day, and the carpenter estimated that at this pace, they would still need all the following morning.

Their situation was growing critical, however. The dead were overwhelming the living with their quickly spreading pestilence. Not two hours would pass now without one of them claiming his place on the forecastle. The rest would hurry to dispose of him. Sometimes they no longer took the time to clean the plank when blood or pus leaked through the canvas shroud. They had abridged the funeral ceremony (Girandole was in charge, since Bloche no longer left his cabin except for meals), but they never forgot to weight the sack with its two six-pound shot, for there was now an entire cemetery twenty-five fathoms beneath the vessel, and they dreaded seeing one of its inhabitants return to the surface. This anxiety preyed on them so fiercely that some of the men had approached Girandole, offering to take the bodies out to sea on the large raft for burial. He had agreed, and the first of these convoys was the worst, for it carried the cabin boy, whose remains, sprinkled with vinegar, had given off a stomach-turning stench. At first the crew took the raft a long way before tipping the body over the side, but the frequency of these trips soon diminished their zeal. They decreased the distance, and then decided not to go out unless they had a double load.

In any case, it was an exhausting task, and not many of the men were now fit to undertake it. Most of the crew still on their feet were incapable of pulling at the oars for an hour—indeed, they were incapable of any sustained effort. All these dejected souls spent their time collapsed in corners with their mouths hanging open, staring gloomily at nothing. Obsessed by food, they came to life only to eat and drink. They waited for their spoiled rations and fouled water with such frantic eagerness that Bloche and Girandole, fearing possible depredations, decided to forbid access to the hold. Once the materials necessary for the construction of the raft had been brought up, they armed a few gunners and posted them at the foot of the ladders, with the warning that they would be held responsible for even the slightest theft.

The rain, in quenching their thirst, had revived and cheered the men. It had been a day of blessings, an answer to their prayers made in the spirit of the wise proverb: God helps those who help themselves.

For during the afternoon, they had found a way to take the edge off their hunger, while at the same time relieving some of the strain on their nerves.

The ship was now overrun with rats. Unaffected by the desolation, fit, frisky, and in finest fettle, they grew bolder and more pugnacious as the men languished. It was not unusual to see them trotting cheekily out in the open or even bristling at a sailor's challenge. Their sinister, invasive presence distressed the men, who felt the rodents were drawn by the scent of death, awaiting their chance at the spoils. After the cabin boy's fate became known, everyone had the odious sensation of being watched, hungrily, as potential prey.

Perhaps that is how things would have remained if it had not been for Brousseau. His companions had been allowed to keep him between decks on condition that he be under restraint. They had tied one of his wrists to a stanchion. He gave them no trouble, usually sitting motionless with his eyes glazed, occasionally muttering a few words to which no one listened. He was not bothered by the rats, some of which even came close enough to sniff at his feet. This time, inexplicably, he snatched up a passing rat and squeezed it in his fist. Cruelty or hunger had lighted up his eyes. When the rat did not die fast enough to suit him, he bit into its throat with his remaining yellow teeth. He lapped at the oozing gore as though it were goat's milk. When his mates tore the animal from his bloody grasp, he was furious.

"I wasn't finished!" he shouted.

Once their initial revulsion had passed, some of the men began to see that ball of gray fur in a more appealing light.

Not everyone decided to eat rat, but even the squeamish were willing to join in the pursuit, since it cost them nothing to kill as many of these pests as possible. The chase was on, *sans brio*. The men's former liveliness was long gone. Running set them wheezing, and their cudgel blows fell wide. Four or five hunters would close in on their quarry only to see it dart between their legs. Nevertheless, on that first evening they had bagged enough to serve each man a half a rat at supper—even at the captain's table, for the gentlemen had not turned up their noses at this fresh meat. Dressed, the animal proved rather disappointing: its plumpness carved down to a tiny saddle and two diminutive drumsticks; but when the cook had finished with them (Frichoux, the baker, more expert at preparing such delicacies, was wasting away in the sick bay), the fricassee tasted quite simply like rabbit, and there were no complaints.

Their hunting instincts revived, the men had been eyeing other vultures as well: birds, lured down from the skies to hover overhead, drawn by the appetizing odor of corpses. Most of them circled high above the ship. Some, however, were bold enough to land near a shrouded body lying on the almost deserted deck. They would take three steps, heads up, then attack the canvas with nervous pecks, constantly stopping to look warily about with their staring round eyes. They rarely had enough time to taste the decomposing flesh before a man on watch gave the alarm.

The famished crew remembered their earlier attempt to shoot the birds. Now they had an added advantage: the raft, which could fetch any birds that fell into the water. They also calculated, somewhat cynically, that the corpses would attract plenty of game. The chevalier declined their proposition. Girandole considered it indecent, but did not oppose the plan. It was Colinet who agreed to lie in wait with a musket.

After an hour, he killed one bird. That was all. The gunshot put the rest to flight for the remainder of the day.

Early next morning the sea was still restless, and the sky was smeared with a milky haze. In the distance, silvery fish began wriggling in a frenzy at the surface. Three patients had died during the night.

All morning long, the men worked on the second raft, finishing it only by the afternoon. It was then launched immediately. The four-man party was ready to go: Colinet, who had accepted his assignment with the swaggering air of a young hussar; Lesur and La Bigorne, two eager volunteers; and the chevalier, the last to go aboard. Six sailors commanded by Vallier were on the larger raft, which had been loaded with a few empty casks, some ropes and grapnels, as well as iron bars they intended to fix on the reef as mooring posts.

The convoy set out at four o'clock. The sun had broken through the tattered clouds, some of which seemed to rocket up into the sky. The air now had a sharp, acid quality that brought out the slightest details of the island. The men could just imagine each glossy leaf, each palm frond, each fruit; they glimpsed the brilliant spangles of the waterfall, the reflections on the gleaming rocks, the tangled network of succulent bushes clinging to the slopes; they saw each treetop in the fleecy green covering of the hillocks, and the almost black outline of the highest branches against the sky; they counted the rings on the coconut palm trunks, the detours of the ravines through the mossy meadows, the red flowers in the violet shadows, the long, spiky stalks of the traveler's trees with their compound leaves, rippling like ribbons in the slightest breeze. It was a scene of pristine beauty.

The convoy rowed to within a cable's length of the breakers. What had seemed from the ship like a gentle lapping of foam was in fact a powerful, frothing sea that fell upon the reef in rumbling waves and geysers of white water. Determined though he was, Colinet felt it was impossible to draw any closer. Still, he wanted there to be no mistake about the matter. Two of the sailors on the large raft had gone on its first voyage, and Colinet called out to them.

"Did Monsieur Malestro jump into such a rough sea as this?"

The sailors replied that he had not, that the water had been much calmer.

"Do you think he would venture in today?" added Colinet naïvely, in the uneasy anticipation of later seeing his courage compared with Malestro's.

He heard the sailors' answer with relief: Malestro would have turned back, as would anyone else, no matter how good a swimmer he was. In any case, no one would even dream of attempting to swim…

They approached to within ten toises of the barrier. Capricious currents, added to the swell, were tossing the rafts about, preventing them from drawing any closer without the risk of capsizing. Before them lay breakers waiting to drive men and rafts upon the rocks and batter them to pieces.

Suddenly, a powerful lurch knocked Colinet off his feet, sending him rolling across the platform and beneath the manrope. He pitched overboard, headfirst. Dashing after him, the chevalier managed to grab his leg as he was going under. Lesur and La Bigorne rushed over. Together they hauled Colinet from the water. Everything had happened so quickly that he had had no idea what was happening to him. He was unhurt, but had lost his tricorn, his wig, and much of his jaunty manner. He agreed with the chevalier that it was not only impossible to pull alongside the reef but also quite dangerous to stay in its vicinity. The convoy swung around and returned to the *flûte*.

*

The entire expedition had taken less than an hour. The men on the ship had seen everything, guessed everything. Slobbering, toothless, covered with abscesses, their hair coming out in patches, riddled with decay, their faces twisted into masks of distress, they whimpered pitifully. The blessings of the rain had gone, and all hope with them. Misfortune had not loosened its grip after all. Yes, the island was there before their eyes, with its fruits, its sweet water, and its heavenly shade. Within musket range was enough and to spare of happiness, and goat's milk, too, perhaps. But for whom? What was the use of drooling over it? Because all that spittle was from sheer longing! It was damned torture, more cruel than an empty sea. There they might have grappled with their fate, confronted their despair without this deafening siren song. Wasn't it all a laughable mistake, a foolish nightmare? Idiot! Try laughing when your belly's kissing your backbone! No, it was no dream. A wall stood between the ship and the island, a wall more terrible than the coral reef, a wall between heaven and hell. Was it impassable? Had Girandole perhaps failed in his mission? Wasn't there one opening somewhere? Or ten, or twenty? There simply had to be...They should go see. They had to escape from this place. But challenging the coral rock was madness...Confound it! Anything was better than waiting for death!

Scurvy continued its ravages: three dead that morning, two in the afternoon. There were thirty-five men on the sick list. The bosun Baudin, his mate Lagarde, and the sailmaker Guyader were among them. Coridan and Dominique were at death's door. Trinquet had taken to his bed as well, too weak to take his meals with the others anymore. And Bloche was not recovering from his illness.

This inexorable increase in the number of patients was bringing Saint-Foin to his knees. Every evening he collapsed onto his bunk without bothering to take off his shoes and slept as one dead. This profound fatigue could blot out his sufferings for a few hours, after which he had to seek relief from belladonna or mandrake root, or even poppy syrup. Sleep had become so precious to him that he no longer wished to be awakened in the event of a patient's final agony and death. Robinot—who slept in his own peculiar fashion, in little snatches, as quick to drop off as he was to snap awake again—took care of the corpse with the help of two or three men fetched from on deck. Saint-Foin would count the shrouded figures the next morning. Then he would return to his duties, with no illusions.

"How wide of the mark we are!" he thought. "Do our remedies give these wretches even one more day of life? When a few fruits and fresh vegetables would be enough to cure them! What is our entire pharmacopoeia against a single fruit? I shall not save any of them. 'Tis the island that will save them, or else we are all lost. The remedies are there, on terra firma. The sea is inhuman. Man cannot live without trees and their fruits…"

Only one patient gave him satisfaction, and that was

Malestro, who was showing uncommon resilience against the effects of the poison. Simarouba bark had never before brought down a fever so quickly. The pain in his leg, which had at first extended all the way up to the groin, had gradually retreated to the foot and calf. He still had a large pink swelling on his ankle, but a treatment of Goulard's extract and alum had prevented the wound from turning septic. The patient was already furious at not being able to walk yet.

When Saint-Foin had looked in on him at the end of that afternoon, Malestro had already heard about the failure of the expedition. Nervously, almost irritably, he asked the surgeon if there were plans to send the rafts out again, if other ideas were being considered, if there had been a change in the weather, if even the slightest breeze had come up. He sensed only uncertainty and resignation in the surgeon's replies.

"Saint-Foin, for the love of God! Get a grip on yourself. This island is not inviolable. Men have set foot on her, and I believe I know how they did so."

Though pressed by the surgeon, Malestro would tell him no more.

"Later. First, be so kind as to obtain a crutch for me. I should like to go see the captain. Unless Bloche would consent to come to me, which, after all, would require no more than twenty-five steps or so."

Saint-Foin promised to transmit the request and left, reflecting that this devil Malestro might well be their last hope before death got the better of them. As he made his

way to the great cabin, he suddenly imagined a ship—
silent, immobile, strewn with skeletons picked clean by
rats, a ship now free of howling rage and terror,
immersed in a boundless peace once briefly troubled by a
handful of men. He considered this strange vision with a
kind of acceptance, but only for a moment.

"Not so fast!" he exclaimed. "You have not heard the
last of us yet!"

An hour later, Bloche entered Malestro's cabin. He had
put on his black cloth waistcoat and a wig that was a trifle short. Instead of his familiar high boots, he was wearing buckled shoes, which made his feet seem quite small.
His face was deathly pale, his cheeks flabby, his skin dry;
his breath came in short, shallow gasps. He sank into
an armchair, crossed his great hams, and inquired carelessly after the other man's health. Then he came to the
point.

"So. You wanted to see me. Here I am. According to
Saint-Foin, you say you know of a way to reach the
island. I am listening."

Malestro moved his leg slightly, winced, and began to
speak.

"Well, Captain, at first I thought our simplest course
would be to cross over the coral. I know this can be done,
but only in a smooth, quiet sea. In any case, others have
been here before us, and I doubt they came that way."

"What others? Do you still believe in that fantastical
goat? Or are you thinking of the brigantine?"

"And why not?"

"But that old hulk never made it through the channel, is that not so?"

"Who can say? The fire may have done for her when she was coming in or going out—either way. But 'tis no matter. These are not necessarily the people who have landed on this island."

"Who, then?"

"Others."

"How do you know?"

"I have proof. Do not ask me to say more."

"None of that, Malestro! This is not the moment."

"Captain, the question is of no importance. This is what matters. Those on the brigantine were right to enter the channel, for there is but a single passage along the entire coast: that one."

"Agreed, but where does it go? The bay is bounded by impregnable escarpments."

"Impregnable for a boat or a raft—not for a ship."

"Explain yourself!"

"The masts, Captain. Climbing to the top of the masts, one would be high enough to toss grapnels upon the small shoulders not too far above. Then it would be enough to let the ropes hang down the rock face so that men might grasp them, from a raft or swimming in the water, and haul themselves up."

"I see. There remain, however, two sizable obstacles. The first is the wreck blocking the channel."

"We blow her to blazes."

"Dammit! You would have us go all out, monsieur."

"We must. The wood is charred, and cannonballs will

blast it to smithereens."

" 'Twill not be enough. The pieces will hinder our passage."

"They will sink. Mid-channel is twenty fathoms deep."

"Let us assume what you say is true. Cannonballs will not remove the other obstacle, however. How would you have the *flûte* proceed to the channel? If you intend to pull her with the rafts, 'twould be better if you gave this plan up straightaway."

"I know…A good wind would surely save us."

"What wind? There is not so much as a fart."

"All we need is to reach that current out at sea. If you recall, we crossed it while pulling the ship. It leads to the channel. Do you not think that with a kedge anchor…"

Bloche sat up defiantly.

"Do you propose to let the ship drift in the current?"

"Yes."

"Impossible!"

"Why?"

"She would be uncontrollable."

"For a time. The current is not dangerous…"

"And the reefs, and the shallows—what of them? We should be helpless to keep from being driven into them."

"There do not seem to be any in the set of this current."

"How do you know? You are talking nonsense, Malestro. You put me in mind of the chevalier, who is all for simply running the ship upon the coral."

"Well? Would you rather she served as our coffin?"

"As coffins go, I would at least have the planks."

"A poor advantage."

"Oh! This ship has greater ones. In particular—and you seem to have forgotten this—it is our only way home. I shall not endanger her, Malestro. Never in life, do you hear me! I am quite willing to consider your plan, but understand this! As long as we do not have enough wind to give the ship steerageway, she will not budge from here."

Malestro stared in silence at the big man, who was now breathing hard.

"As you wish," he said finally, narrowing his green eyes ever so slightly.

XIII.

It WAS ONE O'CLOCK in the morning when the end of a rope was tossed out of a porthole and left dangling. A man slipped through the narrow opening, grasped the line, and slid down to the small raft. The movement of the sea in the darkness was visible only in the blue phosphorescence that bloomed along the hull. Standing on the heaving platform, the man gave the rope a light tug and whistled softly. Another man emerged from the porthole, but with more difficulty. Twisting, puffing, and groaning, he finally pulled himself through and slid down to join his companion, who then called up in a hushed voice.

"Ahoy, Espinglet! Heave it down."

A keg appeared in the opening, tied to some rope-yarn, and descended jerkily to the two men. They seized it and untied the knot.

"Haul away!" ordered the same man.

The rope disappeared. Soon another keg was lowered.

Then a third. Finally, Espinglet thrust his head out.

"Your turn," they called from below. "Come on."

He began to climb out. He was thin, and had no diffi-culty, but suddenly, halfway out the porthole, he froze.

"My word!" intoned a deep voice. "The rats are leaving the ship."

The men on the raft stood motionless as well, peering upward. They were caught. Their companion, however, reflected that he might still escape unnoticed by drawing back into his hole. For the moment, he decided to remain stock-still, his eye on La Bigorne and Ramberge.

To their relief, however, the two gunners had recog-nized Malestro in the feeble light of a nearby lantern, leaning over the rail in his shirtsleeves with what looked like a roll of papers under his arm. It was the pad of a crutch.

"Idiots!" he hissed, lowering his voice. "And here I am, breaking my back to save you. Haul up your wretched baggage. We have better things to do."

Now that their hearts had stopped pounding, the two men below were amazed to see that devil back on his feet when they had thought him prostrate with fever and pain. They resented being thrown into a cold sweat by his unexpected appearance and carefully hid their surprise.

"That's what you say," replied one of them. "As for us, we're heading out to sea. We'll not croak here. Come along, if you like."

"Not so fast, Ramberge!" said Malestro. "Do not take that familiar tone with me! You are not out of reach yet.

One word from me and you would be clapped into irons."

"What're you waiting for?"

"Do you think I would hesitate one moment? I was looking for you. I will perhaps have need of you. If you desert, you betray me. Try it and I swear I will have you shot."

Hearing a sound along the side of the ship, he leaned farther over the rail and saw the shadow of the third thief, halfway out the port and trying to wriggle back inside.

"And that one there, who is he?"

"'Tis nobody," said La Bigorne.

"Well, I advise you to come back, the way he is so wisely doing. You will join me up here. There is no one about…So, gentlemen, I am waiting!"

La Bigorne turned to Ramberge.

"He has convinced me," he said sarcastically. "That man loves us dearly. 'Twould break his heart was we to abandon him. D'you not think so?"

Then he grasped the line and climbed back up.

Shortly afterward, three men stood together on deck, away from the scattered sleepers with their sighs and moans. Malestro was leaning back against a bulwark, his right foot set on a coil of rope. The boot was slashed open at the ankle and plugged with a wad of cloth. He spoke briefly to his listeners about his plan, the captain's disapproval, and the chevalier's subsequent interest.

"Du Mouchet favors it wholeheartedly," he said. "He went below directly to discuss it with Bloche. Without success. He returned in an evil humor."

"What happened?"

"Ah, our deserter wishes to be made privy to the doings of his betters?"

"And why not? You're the one as had me climb back on board, so I trust it weren't for nothing. Now then, what did they say?"

"Bloche is in a bad way. He told the chevalier straight out he wished to resign in favor of Girandole. Du Mouchet replied that in such a case, he would prefer to take command himself. Which surprised our dear captain, who immediately smelled a rat. When the chevalier revealed his intention to carry out my plan, Bloche flew into a temper, declaring he would not resign after all and would hear no more about it. Things went from bad to worse. Du Mouchet will likely relieve Bloche of his duties. Should he shrink from this, however, I shall then have need of you."

"What for?"

"How many men might we count on? If they may still be called men…"

The two old hands understood instantly.

"Avast, there!" cried La Bigorne. "What d'you mean to drag us into?"

"Now is not the time to get cold feet," replied Malestro. "Were you not about to rush headlong into a very bad business indeed? Put your minds at ease: I merely consider a possibility, no more. Surely it will not come to that. Du Mouchet is bold enough to undertake this affair."

"What of it?" observed Ramberge. "'Twould have been simpler to slip away on the raft."

"I need the *flûte*."

"We don't."

"You have but one eye, and not much brain. And I have more pressing things to do than try to talk some sense into you. Either you are with me—or I denounce your attempt at desertion with those kegs of pilfered provisions straightaway."

Ramberge turned in indignation to his companion, who remarked resignedly, "You see, I told you: if we was to leave, he'd never get over it."

Malestro's precautions proved unnecessary. By ten o'clock the following morning, it was all over. After one last meeting with the captain, the chevalier had relieved him of his command. Girandole had declared his support for Bloche and demanded—quite impertinently—to be removed from his post. His wish was granted: he was placed under arrest. When chosen to replace him, Colinet was briefly troubled with qualms of conscience, which vanished as soon as he accepted the position. As for Saint-Foin, he sided immediately with the chevalier.

"Now, monsieur," he urged him, "you must act, and quickly!"

One hour later, the twenty or so men still on their feet had assembled in the waist. Standing behind the barricade, flanked by Malestro and Colinet, the Chevalier Du Mouchet announced that he had assumed command of the ship. He then described the course of action he had decided to take. Wearing his wig and a simple linen waistcoat crossed by the shoulder belt of his sword, his face pale and puffy, he looked as though he were about to fight a duel after a night of debauchery. On his right, Colinet stood stiffly, correctly attired from head to toe, while on his left, Malestro resembled a pirate in his old coat of bronze velvet and his slashed boot, a crutch jammed under his arm and a pistol in his belt.

Once they had recovered from their surprise, the men were willing to agree that this so-called commander, who had hardly counted for much until then, was finally taking his role seriously. They had no complaints. On the contrary—was he not offering to pull them out of this hellhole?

The chevalier announced that he was naming Colinet first mate, that Vallier would remain the bosun, while La Bigorne and Ramberge were promoted to bosun's mates. (This last measure had of course been suggested by Malestro, who thought it wise, on the whole, to consolidate his position.) Then Du Mouchet put Colinet in charge of maneuvering the ship.

The men went to the capstans, shipped the bars, and set to. They had first to weigh the bower and the sheet anchor. They labored away, but with such difficulty that it was almost an hour before they were done.

Then they had to warp the ship around and bring her into the current. The kedge anchor was loaded onto the small raft and dropped with its buoy at a distance, so that they might move the vessel by hauling in the cable. Squatting in the water, the ship swung around only grudgingly, like a yoke of oxen. The *flûte*, like the men, seemed to have

lost the habit of motion. This inertia did not help the
sailors, who wore themselves out heaving at the capstan
bars. Sometimes one of the men would drop from exhaustion, and the others would step right over him.

At one o'clock, the ship was finally facing the open sea.
The bell struck a very late dinner, which the men welcomed with relief.

Once their burning fatigue had subsided, they ate in
high spirits. With the chevalier's permission, Malestro
had had wine and tafia brought up from the hold, along
with entire casks of salt cod. Instead of dining on the
skimpy portions of fresh meat provided by the rats, all
hands—including those on the sick list—now feasted on
this plenty. It was a measure designed to put some heart
into them and to win favor for the new command.

In the midst of these festivities lay two shrouded
corpses whose stink mingled with the smell of cod. No
one cared. They well knew that death was still the order
of the day, but from now on they meant to treat it with
contempt, mockery, indifference—in brief, they did not
intend to give in. This sickly blood running through their
veins had begun to boil again, heated by effort and the
wine. These scraps of men stuffed themselves, swaggered
about, prepared for combat with the haughty bluster of
buccaneers. They had forgotten the taste of their suppu-
rating gums.

They returned to their warping, but with short-lived
ardor: the wine had muddled their heads and sapped
their strength. All afternoon long, however, the kedge

was dropped, the hawser wound in, the anchor cast farther out, and the jeer-capstan kept up its constant complaint. It took them five kedgings to warp the ship into
the current, which she reached at six o'clock. The flow
was very weak, and did not move the vessel right away. It
was only after long minutes that the bow began to swing
imperceptibly to port. Gradually, she came round, rocking deeply, and settled into a current of which the men
could see no trace. And there she seemed to sit. Later,
toward nightfall, by lining up some landmarks, they realized she was making slight headway. They left her to it...

The night air was mild and fragrant; even though the
ship had long since left her cesspool behind, she had had
to come some distance to breathe once more the wonder-
ful smell of the sea. As darkness fell, the chevalier had
quit the deck. Although the *flûte* was gliding peacefully
through these unknown waters, borne by the current, he
knew how deceptive this peace was. There was nothing
more for him to do, however, but to abandon himself to
the seductive pleasure of drifting along. He had gone to
his cabin to splash his face with water, and then, before
going to supper, he had stopped to visit Trinquet.

The old man was lying down; his breathing was
labored. He could no longer see and dabbed constantly
with a handkerchief at the purulent matter discharged
from his eyes. A servant had lighted the little hanging
lamp anyway. The chevalier touched the end of his cigar
to the flame to rekindle the ember.

They talked. Cornelius scolded him about what he called the mutiny and warned him to watch out for Malestro. He was not worried about the venture—indeed, he was in favor of it. Du Mouchet discounted his opinion, knowing how little the old man knew of navigation and how liable he was to scoff at the greatest perils when anxious to reach some destination or other.

A servant brought Trinquet his supper. He sat up on his cushions and began to eat, fumblingly, but refusing any help. He had stopped talking, and as he chewed, he rolled his chin around in circles.

The chevalier respected his silence. He smoked. Memories filled his thoughts. He recalled the old man's search, from island to island, from tribe to tribe, for anything that would help him in his stubborn pursuit of the legend of that vast land mass. The chevalier could still clearly recall one place where Trinquet's quest had led him. It was a small, mountainous country they had reached by winding through a series of low islands so flat they were almost awash. Squalls and sudden downpours had drenched the *Entremetteuse* relentlessly. He remembered that during one of those storms a man had fallen overboard and they had been powerless to save him.

Relying on the information he had already gathered, Cornelius had expected much from that visit. He had eagerly disembarked among the dumbfounded natives. The first ones he questioned, after the customary bumpers of wine, had not completely satisfied him with their answers, for although they seemed to have a precise idea of the great land he was describing, they were reluctant to speak of it. They advised him to consult a wise old man who lived apart from their village, and agreed to provide a guide to take him there.

The chevalier remembered the evening when Picot-Fleury, Malestro, and he had set out with Trinquet at around six o'clock, led by a child less than twelve years old. After climbing an interminable path, they arrived at a hut of branches standing in the middle of a grove of dry, dusty trees. In what passed for a yard, a big, naked black woman seated on a block of wood was busy plucking a large white bird, and her huge breasts were snowy with feathers. Alerted by the child, the old man had emerged from his hut to speak with them. He was as smooth as a peeled twig. His only garment was a small square woven of thin strips of material worn over the lower part of his abdomen.

Trinquet offered him a broad ax, a comb, a medal, some nails, and a length of silk. The old man refused each gift in turn. He then accepted a large feather of a brilliant red color, but handed it back after examining it, speaking a few brisk words to the fat woman as he did so and giving a short, husky laugh.

Cornelius explained why he had come, and the old man seemed to understand. He responded with clear gestures that said, "Yes, I know this continent, and I know where it lies." (His description of the large land mass left no room for doubt—it was suitably immense.) "Come back in three days, two hours before the setting of the sun" (this was the position he indicated in the sky), "and I will show it to you."

The small band respectfully took their leave and went

off much intrigued by the old man's promise to show them a continent of which not even the slightest stretch of coastline could be seen.

During the next three days, they visited the island, took on wood and water, and traded with the natives. These people were peaceful, pleasant, not much given to stealing, but the women refused in disgust to have anything to do with the visitors, who soon became bored, the chevalier along with everyone else, for they had by then grown used to spicier fare.

When the day came, the four gentlemen were at the rendezvous at the appointed time. In the yard, the spot where the fat woman had been was still littered with white feathers. When they arrived, the old man emerged from his door as he had the previous time, took up a stick, walked around to the back of his hut, and set out without paying any attention to his visitors, who fell in behind him.

Du Mouchet remembered the details of this excursion and the unexpected enjoyment it had given him. Was it the excitement of curiosity or the infinite pleasure of discovering a path, step by step, and believing it to be endless? Even today, he could not tell. They had quickly plunged into a coppice of monkey apple trees, following the faintest of hare tracks; then they had taken a rocky path running by ravines and walls of black boulders. After passing a ridge, they descended immediately into a dense wood, which swallowed them up in shadow. The thick stems of cannas jutted out into the path. Clumps of dragon trees shed clouds of flies and wasps as they brushed past. Every trunk and limb was draped with a parasitic web of vines and leaves. Massive breastplates of greenery were edged with lacy tree ferns. At long intervals, huge mahogany trees loomed amid their Gothic buttresses, occasionally embraced by a voluptuous vine ascending to entangle itself in the branches. The loamy soil cushioned their steps; the humidity muffled all sounds. They heard only their soft footfalls, the chattering of birds, and the creaking of trees. Beneath their shirts, gaping open at the neck, they felt the sting of sweat heavily dusted with pollen.

A sudden cloudburst drenched them, and then the sun returned to polish the vast crowns of foliage. Ahead of them, the silent old man set down his bare feet as though they were hands, with the agility of a monkey and the tranquil endurance of a child. They skirted a ravine, and after passing some cinnamon and gum trees, came upon another coppice of monkey apples, bathed in orange by the low-lying sun. In the distance lay the immense flat basin of the sea. They lost it amid the thickets, and continued their descent.

Finally they came to a sloping piece of ground where only rosemary bushes and white frangipani grew. They saw the sea again, dyed a deep and perfect blue. The sandy waste plunged on ahead and out of sight. They advanced far enough to see below them an immense terrace, dazzling white and shaken by strange tremors. At the same moment, they were struck by the din.

Before their eyes were gathered thousands of jabbering white birds, trembling in a whirl of wings and beaks, covering the terrace with a pelisse of ermine rippling in the wind.

The old man had stopped and stood gazing at the birds. Cornelius, disconcerted, cried, "What does this mean?" Their guide signaled to him to be quiet and wait.

The poppy-red sun was just touching the horizon. With impassive splendor, streaks of jade green marbled the sea and sky. Everything around this quivering flock was vast and serene. The sun sank in silence. The sea was smooth all the way to the shore, edged only with the most delicate milky froth.

The birds grew suddenly still. They remained so for a moment, waiting. Then, in their midst, something began to flutter and spread outward, and this snowy fur cloak rose up as though lifted by a fist. It shivered all over, began to billow, and floated entirely free, a shimmering of wings with a sound like the cracking of whips. Gliding now to one side, now to another, it rose ever higher, then shot out over the sea.

The sun had set. High above, the colony of birds was soon no more than a pinch of salt tossed into the air. The old man looked at Cornelius. He held a long, smooth hand out toward the terrace, gestured as though weighing a purse, and then pronounced a single word. And what this word clearly meant was: continent.

*

In the small wooden room cluttered with papers, where the air still smelled of old clothes and candlewax, the chevalier contemplated his former tutor, who was just finishing his dinner. He could see him yet, returning in a fury from their excursion shouting that he'd been gulled by an old fool, that these natives were jackasses, that he would continue his search without their help... In other words, that he would sail blindly around the boundless ocean. Of course, it was not a needle he was seeking in this haystack. But the sea was inexhaustible. He might have worn out ten ships and ten crews, as he had worn out his eyes, without ever seeing the half of it.

The chevalier could still discern, on that sick and wizened face, the telltale signs of deep conviction. He found this belief absurd. There was nothing out there but islands, irremediably closed and finite. It was hopeless to pursue endless advances into limitless lands. The old native had understood: it was not a question of land, but of taking flight. Du Mouchet did not want to fall into this trap, however; to him it smacked unpleasantly of preaching. To hell with these bursts of airy enthusiasm! As for him, he needed good, solid ground, the carnal, sensual, voluptuous world here below. Never mind that one had to acknowledge its limitations—that was better, all in all, than the emptiness of dreams.

Invigorated by his little meditation, he took a last puff on his cigar and crushed it carelessly beneath his heel. Then he rose to leave.

"Cornelius," he said, "that continent does not exist."

XIV.

THE *FLÛTE* GHOSTED through the night. The squares of light along her sides seemed to announce a celebration, or perhaps a wake. There was something about her of both gaiety and death.

Free to ransack the hold, the crew had invaded the storerooms with lanterns and torches. They had forced locks, smashed open barrels, and dumped out spoiled provisions, through which they now pawed eagerly. It was a pathetic orgy over heaps of garbage. Mavel crouched in front of a little mound of beans, picking out the soundest ones to stash in his cap. A horse-faced red-head crammed biscuits into his mouth, cracking his teeth on them. Others plunged their arms into tubs of salt meat that turned to sludge between their fingers. All sorts of foul and acrid odors, imprisoned until then inside their casks, now overpowered the smell of slime and tar.

Only the wine kept disgust and discouragement at bay.

Broached casks disgorged their red juice into pitchers. The men formed a chain, and some kind souls took jugs up to their mates in the sick bay. The acidic wine dribbling down chins and dripping onto the floor revived memories of tavern revelry, of licentious sprees when women with their blouses all unbuttoned had let themselves be fondled, squealing with raucous delight. Their thighs tingling at the thought, the sailors told themselves they'd have a fine old time in the arms of one of those fat, musky whores whose scent and image they kept hidden away, deep in their hearts.

The pillaging of the stores came to an end before midnight. Scurvy had ruined their endurance. A few fell asleep on the spot, amid the sour fumes of spoilage, wine, and vomit. Laden with provisions, the others went topside one by one. There they collapsed, but did not fall asleep. They sat dreaming, killing the putrid taste of their saliva with little swigs of tafia. The drink had put some guts into them. They felt on their mettle once again, and discovered, with secretly renewed pride, that nothing could frighten them anymore, not their bodies, or their fate, or the pitch-dark night with its lurking reefs, or the moans of their sick mates unsilenced by the wine, or the corpses of Frichoux and Mâche-fer wrapped in their shrouds, or, lying next to them, the body of young Dominique, whose pretty peach-fuzz cheeks were fast falling into decay. Their souls floated free of these horrors. They would cheerfully have bedded a colony of lepers. They gazed up into the starry sky with its dark scraps of scudding clouds and believed that a stout heart would protect them from death.

The gentlemen aboard had drunk their fill of finer liquors, but their spirits were soaring to similar heights. Even Bloche and Girandole—made quite tipsy through the ministrations of Malestro—had abandoned much of their hostility. Although they still condemned the undertaking, they now regarded it more fatalistically as they recovered from the shock of their removal. They were no longer concerned about the depletion of the provisions. They felt these stores would soon be useless, whether they themselves were at the bottom of the sea or clinging to some makeshift buoy. They were resigned, unlike the others, which made their cool demeanor all the more creditable. Their intoxication helped—as did, perhaps, a glimmer of hope they secretly cherished as well.

The chevalier was also burning through his reserve: he had smoked four cigars since nightfall. At midnight, he lit up a fifth as he went out onto the stern-gallery carrying a glass of rum. The ship had drawn closer to the island, which was full of noises, thousands of soft chirrings that together outplayed the rumble of the breakers. The endless song ran down along the hills to the shore. The island was murmuring gently. The chevalier could see nothing but a great black mass, but she was there, quite close by. He thought he could smell her perfumed warmth. He could almost touch her. Now he breathed in the scent of sand and shells. There was a faint tart odor of bruised leaves, and then the lightest fragrance of cinnamon. His nostrils quivered. He was wide awake and wholly given over to the pleasure of this slow approach. He smoked his cigar as though it were his last. Tomorrow, he would be prepared to exhaust his reserve of tobacco, the last stores in the hold—indeed the ship herself! A plague on baggage! The island would satisfy all his hungers.

Dawn unveiled shores of the purest grays. The island had not draped herself in her mists. She was naked.

The ship had rounded the headland and left it behind. Malestro, again claiming to recognize in it the profile of a monkey, had dragged La Bigorne and Ramberge onto the quarterdeck, but they saw nothing more than a misshapen boulder. The ship had also passed densely wooded hills and was now skirting some scattered reefs lying before high escarpments. The *Entremetteuse* drifted silently, rocked by the swell, borne along by the current like a barge. She had well and truly made it through the night without accident, and the men began to believe in their good fortune. Only Bloche, who had awakened in a less peaceable mood, was unconvinced.

"'Tis a miracle," he snapped to his servant. "We shall not get another one."

While down in the hold some men were still deep in a feverish sleep, others up on deck opened one eye, tasted the milky air of dawn, and turned their faces to the cliffs. Looking out over the bows, they glimpsed the little island across from the bay, and several hearts beat faster at the sight. They clucked tongues that tasted of ashes and crab, scratched their stiff and mangy hides, rubbed their spiky shocks of hair, and began to see about quenching their thirst.

Meanwhile, Du Mouchet had brought Malestro and Colinet to his cabin to discuss the difficult maneuver ahead. Since the current passed to seaward of the islet, the ship had to break free of it and proceed to the entrance of the channel, there anchor, and bombard the wreck. Malestro, whose jaw was shadowed with coal-black stubble, presented his plan to Colinet, with one precautionary remark.

"As I am not a sailor, you may well find some fault with it."

It was a delicate business, but Lieutenant Chicken Coop had not lost any of his customary bravado. He had acquitted himself very well the day before, with Vallier's support. Now he listened and made only a few well-chosen comments, exactly what was needed to reassure the chevalier and Malestro. Colinet took his leave. Shortly afterward, all hands were called on deck.

Mustering them took some time, as there were still men in the belly of the ship. Vallier, La Bigorne, and Ramberge had to go below with lanterns. They found three wine-stained sleepers in the spirit room, where they had been drinking straight from the spigot. The revelers were much annoyed at being roused by a kick in the ribs. Another fellow was snoring in a room full of trade goods; he had opened chests, scattered their contents, and decked himself out in trinkets before passing out amid the muslins and baubles. The gunner Bignon came dashing up all by himself: some rats, taking him for dead or dying, had been licking their lips over him and had awakened their intended prey with their tickling. He drooled and rolled his walleyes, still trembling from the fright that had sent him leaping up in the air to run for his life. The searchers had to give up on the last few—two or three, they hardly knew—who were holed up somewhere, were not answering when hallooed, and were perhaps dead of apoplexy and already nibbled by the rats. Vallier left them a lantern hanging in the central passageway, and all returned topside, the men herded along by the petty officers and grumbling as they went.

After taking soundings and finding coral rock at forty fathoms, Colinet ordered first the bower and then the sheet anchor dropped to port, on the landward side. The first bit. The second dragged, and they felt the ship slow as her stern swung heavily to seaward. Colinet had the sheet anchor brought in until it gripped as well.

A kedge was then loaded onto the small raft, which set out toward the reefs. The sea was breaking too strongly upon them for the men to approach. They struggled with the swirling currents and ended by dropping the anchor and its buoy ten toises from the first line of rocks. The capstan began turning again; the anchor held.

Now they attempted to trip the landward anchors. The bower was raised without any trouble. The other, however, would not come home. While the *flûte* slipped slowly athwart the current, the men heaved in vain upon the bars. For a moment, there was a loud shrieking of wood and hempen rope. Colinet urged the men on. It was no use. Finally, at the repeated insistence of Vallier, he ordered the cable cut.

They were then able to warp the ship to a spot between the reefs and the current. By this time, it was close to ten o'clock. They were now about four cables' lengths from the small island and the entrance to the channel. These long and exhausting maneuvers with the anchors had seriously tired the men. It was impossible, however, to leave the ship floating freely in less than six fathoms of lively water so close to the reefs.

They had to raise the kedge at once by its buoy line and drop it well off the bow. This meant sending out the raft and heaving at the capstan yet again, which brought the ship, a good two hours later, to the mouth of the channel, thirty toises from the islet and a cable's length from the wreck. Here they anchored.

To his chagrin, Malestro found the sea going quite a bit higher than it had on his first visit. The swell sent breakers running pell-mell through the pass to crash upon the skeleton of charred wood. The sunlight gleamed upon these snowy bursts of spray and warmed the towering walls of the bay beyond. Now more than ever, there was a savage grandeur about the place. Frigates swooped and plunged in wild abandon, but all eyes were on a single marvel: high on the rock face, the streamlet had swollen, and its fresh, sweet water, now cascading down in torrents, was only a gunshot away.

Their fatigue had vanished. They forgot the pain throbbing in their limbs. They no longer saw the corpses lying on the deck. It was impatience that tormented them the most. They urged the gunners to cut their dinners short and proceed to the task at hand. Lesur and his three mates—Ramberge among them, for bosun's mate or not, he had decided to help out—were no less excited. After downing some ship's biscuit and wine, they brought shot and cartridges topside and loaded one of the guns in the waist. Everyone was lined up on the port side. Those lying ill between decks had dragged themselves to the portholes; in the sick bay, patients peered out the scuttles along with Saint-Foin and Robinot. Even Bloche had left his cabin, and with the aid of Girandole, had come out onto the gallery to watch.

The preparations took place amid a respectful silence. When his mates had measured out the powder and maneuvered the tackles, Lesur carefully fixed the position of the gun breech with a quoin. Then Ramberge applied the linstock to the touchhole. The cannon roared and belched out thick black smoke.

The ball hit the center of the wreck, sending pieces of it flying. Despite the applause of his audience, Lesur did not want to rejoice too soon.

"A lucky hit," he observed. "This target is a sieve."

They fired again, and this time, as he had feared, the projectile passed clean through the carcass. A third ball fared no better.

"I need bar shot," said the gunner. "Bignon, Garaudel, take some men and fetch me some. You'll see! I mean to chop this woodpile into splinters."

Shortly afterward, the men filled the garland with bar

shot: two cannon balls joined together by an iron bar. The cannonade began anew. From then on, two out of three shots hit their mark.

The gunfire was answered by the echo from the bay and the sudden rending of wood. The thunder reverberated as though enclosed within the nave of a cathedral— a thunder of desecration, accentuated by the infernal reek of dense, bitter smoke and black powder. In the mounting excitement, the men felt a fierce desire to break through, destroy, punch their way through doors. They greeted every hit with jubilant cries. In the tops, up on deck, below decks, everyone was both gun and cannonball. Every last man was carried away by elation. Even Bloche had been caught up in the game.

"Dammit! That devil Lesur can lay a gun like no one else. You watch—he will shift her."

The cannon blasted away for an hour. The wreck was collapsing in shuddering jerks, with sinister cracking sounds. Shards of black wood now heaved on the swell. The big pieces of oak sank as soon as they hit the water.

Finally, after one last, long crack, the remains of the brigantine disappeared. A cheer rose from the ship as the chewed-up wreckage slipped beneath the surface, engulfed by onrushing waves. Some men embraced, others tossed their caps on high, and one tall old sailor spat out his quid and crossed himself.

"Monsieur," said Colinet to the chevalier, "I fear that this sea is going too high for what we have left to do... Should we not, in the meantime, send a raft to the waterfall?"

Du Mouchet, his shirt open, was nervously smoking his cigar. Colinet was struck by the ardent gleam in his black eyes.

"No! Go on!" he exclaimed passionately. "Into the channel, Colinet! Now!"

To move the ship, they had to warp her once again, and this time it was the larger, stronger raft that set out with the kedge into the eddies and boils of the pass. La Bigorne was in command of the five rowers, who struggled for control against waves that hurled them forward, thrust them back, and swept them from side to side. The men managed to make progress, however, and were half a cable's length away when they slued suddenly sideways on the crest of a wave. Those on the ship saw her oars pinwheeling in the air. Then another crest hit them broadside, lifting the raft. A man was tipped overboard. There was a flurry of commotion. While some of the men tried to help by holding their oars out to their drowning companion, others unshackled the anchor, hoping to get rid of the cable that was imperiling the raft. The man in the water grabbed an oar. Just as the anchor was freed, a fresh wave struck the platform, tilting it so steeply that all upon it were flung off.

The raft had fallen back right side up, but out of all its scattered crewmen, not one was able to return to it. Heads were glimpsed above the waves, like floating peppercorns. One by one, they vanished. It was all over in a minute.

Silence had fallen on the ship. Colinet stood speechless

for a moment, then ran to join Du Mouchet, whom he found standing with Malestro. Both men looked grave but determined.

"Monsieur, this is terrible," began Colinet. "We should not have—"

"There is nothing we can do," cut in the chevalier. "Did the kedge anchor bite?"

"I do not know."

"Well, then, go find out."

"But, monsieur! Those poor men! We have just clearly seen how dangerous…"

"What of it?"

"Do you still intend to enter the channel now?"

"Why not? Malestro, your opinion."

Colinet's eyes opened wide at the other man's reply.

"What point is there in waiting? Our anchorage is bad, very bad, and at any instant we may see the anchor come home. If it has gripped the bottom, we should take advantage of this. We shall not be able to drop any others."

"Allow me to—"

"'Tis useless to insist," said the chevalier curtly. "Pray carry out the order, if you please."

The kedge held. The ship entered the churning water at the mouth of the channel, where the sea foamed furiously over the reefs on each side, shooting dazzling plumes into the sunlight. The ebb and flow stirred up great keen-edged crests of polished sapphire that buffeted the vessel. The anchor cable would slacken in an upward rush of

water, and then the underset would pull it suddenly taut,
plunging the ship's rearing bow back into the waves. This
bridle could not last long under such strain. With much
difficulty, the men at the capstan had managed to haul in
half the cable when a rude jolt caused some of its strands
to part as though slashed by a saber. They heaved at the
bars as fast as they could, but it was too late. The next
jolt severed the line.

From now on, the *flûte* was at the mercy of the swell.
She came and went, pitched, rolled, shipped torrents of
warm water that pummeled her crew. Clutching the
quarter rail, the chevalier followed this combat in a state
of exaltation. He felt at one with the ship, pounding like
a battering ram on water as solid as the portals of a
church. Colinet rushed up, his face distorted by fear, and
begged permission to drop another anchor, two, the waist
anchor—but the chevalier sent him back. He was not
afraid. He wanted the ship to have her way.

Despite all this movement to and fro, the *flûte* had
advanced up the channel to the place where the wreck
had lain. But she had gone off course. During one of her
breakneck charges, she struck; the deep sound of the
impact was like the tolling of a gigantic wooden bell. The
ship recoiled, and was swept back into the center of the
channel, slightly athwart the current. She advanced,
gradually, into the pass. Dazed by the sun, the stinging
spray, the racket, and the ferocious bucking of the ship,
the sailors on deck braved this fury with the arrogance of
veteran soldiers under fire. A few shrouded corpses rolled

about on the forecastle deck. Their comrades let them alone, but kept an eye on them, as though they feared one might be awakened by this rude shaking.

The vessel touched again, and several fathoms farther on, crashed violently, bows on, into an invisible wall. A man who had ventured to cross the waist stumbled and ran staggering sideways into a gun carriage. This time, the blow was a fearsome one. Colinet, in despair, clinging to the ship like the others, sent Ramberge and the last caulker below at once to see if she had started a seam.

They were now only thirty toises from the place where the channel widened out. The large raft had already passed through and now rocked in more open waters. Despite the ship's erratic plunging in all directions, she had progressed so far into the channel that those aboard her began to believe they were saved. She struck twice more, and then again, heavily, on the starboard side. And yet, after endless minutes spent squinting at the swell, the reefs, the masts rolling like a pendulum, the grim faces of their companions, and the sun spitting its fire along the top of the cliffs, after praying to all the saints and champing on their quids hard enough to loosen what teeth they had left, after searching for rocks on either side without seeing any more, the men discovered that they had emerged from the passage and entered the bay.

They remained where they were for another moment, frozen in bewilderment. Then they moved carefully to the rails and looked around. The water was as turbulent as it had been in the channel. Cut off from the sun by the top

of the rock wall, the sea was once again mint green. Off
their bows, the large raft was bumping head-on against
the cliff as the swell sent up sprays of lilac-colored water.
In the shade, the waterfall plummeted into a froth of
bubbles, steaming like a kettle on the boil. The men
gazed at it in ecstasy. They were already forgetting the
dangers they had just survived. That was where they
wished to go without delay.

Back in form, and trying to hide his nervous joy, Colinet had soundings taken, let the ship advance another
fifteen toises, and gave the order to heave out the two
bower anchors. The small raft was loaded with casks, and
four men went off to take on water at that mauve spring
gushing from the sky.

Night had fallen upon a still restless sea, its waves coming and going with loud whisperings, while the ship rode
uneasily, tugging on her tethers. Not a breath of wind. A
grumbling sea, and all around, the shrill, trilling sounds
of the island. In the air tumbled heavy bundles of sooty,
oily darkness, fragrant with humus and sweet perfumes.

On the ship, intoxication had come by enchantment.
Great drafts of fresh water—with a taste like the scent
of violets—had been enough to overwhelm the men with
happiness. They wavered between bliss and exuberance.
They spoke repeatedly of their good fortune, the better to
convince themselves of its reality. Yes, the ship was safe.
(They had stopped the leak, a minor one in any case.)
Yes, they had found shelter, in the best of harbors. Yes,

the island was theirs. At the waterfall, the men had even touched the smooth, moist face of the cliff. Tomorrow they would taste the fruits of the island.

Tomorrow…But for some of them, it was too late. Four more had died since that morning. With the six unlucky wretches from the raft, that made ten who had narrowly missed reaching this safe harbor. And there were still three dying men for whom a hundred years would pass before the next day dawned, and whom Saint-Foin and Robinot strove desperately to keep alive. The surgeon lavished care on them: bloodletting, cream of tartar, green powder, Venice treacle, vesicatories…And he administered the poppy syrup with a generous hand, for he could no longer bear to hear them gasp for breath, and felt that pain was harrying them even more quickly to their deaths. He struggled this way until nightfall. Then he ate supper, bending his elbow like the others, before returning to his patients. At eleven o'clock, exhausted and drenched in sweat, he came out into the waist, bareheaded, wiping his neck with a rag.

The men had not been content with their healthy intoxication for long. Their hearts were swelling within their breasts, and demanded stronger stimulants. A handful of the crew had brought jugs of wine and a keg of tafia up from the hold. When the surgeon appeared, one of the tipsiest among them—it was Bat-la-lame—called out to him.

"Major, here's to you! Tonight is a grand night. Let's drink to that. Come over here, Major. You're thirsty, that's plain as day. 'Tis very bad to be thirsty, d'you know that? Come on over, then, you're parched. Drink up, Major. It shan't be said you was the only man not to wet his whistle this night."

Saint-Foin had to admit this was true: everyone, from the great cabin to the sick bay, had been swilling like topers. Even Trinquet had sent for some rum, which he drank in the chevalier's company. Saint-Foin decided that he might well not have anything better to do. He took the mug of tafia held out to him by Bat-la-lame and went off to one side to sit on the edge of a gun carriage. The men had turned back to their own drinking, so he could sip at his mug in peace, massaging his aching abdomen. He was seething with fury inside, and the coarse rum, after the wine at dinner, did nothing to calm him down. He thought about his dying patients.

"No, those three cannot slip away from us now. 'Twould be too cowardly. Yes, cowardly. A man dies when he gives up. 'Tis a weakness of spirit. The body will hold on if the spirit wills it. The body is under orders. Oh, not forever, of course! But right now, what is being asked of it? Barely a few hours. A short while until daybreak..."

He drank his tafia without a care for its rough taste, his nostrils tickled by the lingering odor of gunpowder. A few steps away, the men were speaking by turns in low voices, occasionally bursting out laughing and slapping their thighs. Up on the forecastle, a few corpses lay waiting to be dumped into the sea, their honey-sweet smell drifting down to him now and then. He was drunk enough to put up with it.

"Yes, it would be senseless," he continued. "But does a body have any idea of what is senseless and what is not? Why am I so indignant? Because it would take so little to save them? A little or a lot, what is the difference? That a man dies of scurvy almost within reach of healthful fruits or a thousand miles away, 'tis all the same. It is we who make the distinction, not death. For more than twenty days now we have gazed at this island with our tongues hanging out. Would we have suffered less in the open sea? The body makes its demands blindly. It obtains satisfaction, or it does not. It has no use for temptation, which is a torture of the mind. The body howls, it wants, and when it has had enough of fighting, it scuttles its own ship. Well, then? Are you certain this damned mind is capable of keeping it afloat?…"

His thoughts were interrupted by the sight of Du Mouchet emerging from the main hatchway and unsteadily crossing the quarterdeck. It was not simply that the ship was rolling—the chevalier was drunk. He reached the drift rail, gripped it with both hands, and stared out at the high black walls down which poured all the perfumes of the island. Below, instead of growing quiet, the churning sea was going steadily higher. The chevalier watched the heavy rocking of the ship and seemed to urge on the powerful waves surging around the vessel once again. They were striking more and more violently, with loud spattering sounds. There was something brewing; the chevalier had felt this, and was surrendering to it. Saint-Foin was suddenly afraid.

The Traveler's Tree

*

After pouring floods of tafia down their throats, and finding that rotgut wanting in aroma and character, the men scattered throughout the hold with torches and lanterns headed for the gentlemen's stores. Forcing the locks, they ignored the half-liter bottles of sweet wine and threw themselves upon the kegs of aged rum. Now the precious liquor ran in amber streams across the deck, where they sucked it up into their slobbering, toothless mouths. The fumes alone, in the stifling heat of the room, would have been enough to inebriate them. But there was also the pounding of the sea against the ship's belly, and the hollow thudding of these blows seemed to beat at their own temples. The rum flowed, spangled with gold in the light of the swaying lanterns and torches. Some of the revelers had sat down in the liquor and were soaking their ugly blue calves in it. One of them was singing mournfully. Bourdicaud, the fat bearded man with piggy little eyes, was bubbling over with laughter for no reason, for himself alone. Only someone close enough to peer into those eyes could see that he was sobbing. One man had already collapsed, overcome by drink, his face jammed into his shoulder, his mouth open and pulled to one side. Another man staggered about, throwing his head and shoulders back in an effort to keep his wobbling knees from folding up under him. A sudden and particularly brutal jolt finished him off.

Saint-Foin had been unable to stir from the gun carriage, without understanding the reasons for his terror.

His mind was becoming fuddled. He gazed vacantly from the chevalier to his mug, from his mug to the cluster of drunken sailors. He tried to think clearly, repeating to himself, "After all, I am safe…We are safe…All those who are left will be saved…"

Then he saw Girandole rush out on deck, and hurry over as soon as he spotted him sitting there.

"I was looking for you. The captain has taken a turn for the worse. Come, I beg of you."

Saint-Foin tried to stand up, but a monstrous weight had fallen across his shoulders. He struggled to his feet, his vision blurred by spinning bursts of light. Putting down his mug and rag, he shook himself and set out after the first mate.

Bloche was lying on his bunk, his eyes closed, his breathing shallow. The surgeon immediately unfastened the captain's shirt, baring his powerful chest. The smooth, hairless skin was dotted with tubercles. Saint-Foin put his ear to the man's breast to listen to his heart. Then he lifted the eyelids, felt his forehead, palpated the salivary glands, and examined his legs for signs of edema, without finding any.

"He must be bled," observed the surgeon, turning to Girandole a face clouded with concern. "And this fever must be brought down. I will go to the dispensary at once."

"Would you like me to go instead?"

"No, it would be quicker if I fetched everything. Captain, open your eyes!"

Bloche lifted one eyelid.

"You are not in danger, do you hear me? We will pull you through this, like the rest of us!"

"If you say so," replied Bloche in a thick voice.

Saint-Foin left without bothering to close the door.

Five minutes later, Malestro appeared on the threshold, his crutch under his arm. He was nervous and uneasy. Struck by this unwonted anxiety, Girandole thought at first that Bloche's illness was the cause.

"What do you want?" he cried. "The captain will recover. Saint-Foin should return soon. Leave us."

Malestro paused. He alone—along with Girandole, perhaps, who showed his wine only in the slow blinking of his eyes—seemed to have kept his mind clear. He looked at Bloche, whom he had not expected to find in such a bad way, then back at the first mate.

"You are needed."

"Speak to Colinet."

"He is drunk."

"Who is not?"

"Dead drunk."

"Why do you not join them?"

"Fire has broken out in the hold."

Girandole was seized with alarm.

"What? Where?"

"In the gentlemen's storeroom. Some spilled rum has caught fire."

"God almighty!"

With a glance at the captain, Girandole strode from

the room. Malestro, who had stepped back as the other man passed, now adjusted his crutch and turned to follow him. As he left, he heard Bloche gasp out a few words.

"Drown the powder!…"

In the passageway, they ran into the terrified surgeon, who cried out that there was a fire on board. Approaching the ladder, they saw the first plumes of smoke curling up from the between-decks. Girandole dashed into the waist.

"Vallier! Where is Vallier? Where are his mates?"

Without waiting for a reply or for Malestro, who could not hope to keep up with him, he returned to the ladder and hurried down the first flight. He was heading for the gunners' storeroom, but he saw that efforts to contain the fire were already getting under way there. Still quite groggy and coughing from the smoke, men coming up from the hold were immediately joining the others to collect buckets and carry them topside.

"Where is Vallier?" demanded Girandole again.

"He's getting the fire pump going."

"And the powder magazine, who is taking care of that?"

They did not know. Girandole rushed down the ladder.

The fire had spread smoke and panic through the between-decks. Sick men were howling piteously, and a few had dragged themselves to the door to the waist, where they called for help. No one paid any attention to them. People carrying buckets were running in all directions without managing to form a chain, and the confused shouting of Ramberge only added to the disorder.

Meanwhile, the ship continued to fling herself about in a dizzying ballet of sea foam. Her two anchor cables had broken, one after the other. She was free, and riding on a huge swell. Leaping, plunging, springing forward, then falling all the way back, she was intoxicated with this treacly black water. All her upper works were streaming. And the smoke now pouring from the hatchways seemed to come from this heated rubbing of her belly.

The chevalier still gripped the rail, standing as stiffly as a commander. His drunkenness and the thrashing of the ship had brought on a high fever. His confused thoughts swarmed with scents and images of grass, swamps, sand, leafy shade, vines, thickets, mosses, palm fronds of green leather. He delighted in the ship's battering lunges—and could not understand why. Did he love peace or war? Did he yearn for the land, or for the desire for land? Why, rising and falling with the swell, did he feel so at one with the island? Strange carnal knowledge, this. He did not possess the island. Not yet. He was only urging on his desire, thrusting boldly ahead. Yes, what did he yearn for? Peace? Pleasure? Or perhaps it was all a mirage. No! He was rushing toward it—and one does not rush into a mirage. One believes in it with all one's heart. Yes, he believed in it. And deep down, he needed only to believe in it. What more was there to pleasure than dreaming? Wasn't that what really counted, boldly urging on one's desire?...

He surrendered to his intoxication. This sea tempest was sweeping him away. His blood pounded, and red mists swam before his eyes. There were loud voices now, and hurried footsteps, and a mephitic smell of smoke. He did not turn around. He heard shouts, orders, and from below, a prolonged cry, like the neighing of a horse. Something boiled upward throughout his entire body. Then a massive explosion blew the ship to smithereens.

The carcass and its debris lighted up the walls of the bay. The murmuring of the island had never ceased. The water snuffed out the flickering flames strewn across its surface, one by one, and darkness fell again.

Later, the swell subsided, and the ebb carried off the wreck, leaving it stranded between two reefs. By dawn, the creamy slicks fouling the bay had been swept out to sea. Drifting amid this spume and flotsam was a bottle. It contained only a scrap of paper. Its neck swayed gently from side to side as it floated along. Reaching the current, it set out for Caine.